Loving Her Cowboys

Cowboys Online #3 ~ Moose Ranch

Also by Jan Springer

Club Rendezvous
Shy Girl

Cowboys Online : Moose Ranch
Cowboys for Christmas
Cowboys In Her Pocket
Loving Her Cowboys
Cowboys in Her Heart
Always Her Cowboys

Intimate Secrets
Intimate Lover
Intimate Kisses

Kidnap Fantasies
Jade's Fantasy
Zero To Sexy
Christmas Lovers

Pleasure Bound
A Hero's Welcome
A Hero Escapes
A Hero Betrayed
A Hero's Kiss
A Hero Wanted
Captive Heroes

Pleasure Bound Boxed Set
Pleasure Bound : COMPLETE SERIES SciFi Erotic Romance Boxed Set

Tentacles Shifter Erotic Romance
Taken by Him

The Key Club
A Merry Menage Christmas
Sophie's Menage
Jewel's Menage
Jaxie's Menage

The Outlaw Lovers
Jude Outlaw
The Claiming

Colter's Revenge
Tyler's Woman
Resistance
The Outlaw Lovers
Alpha Outlaws Boxed Set

Vampira
Sweet Heat
Dark Heat
Wet Heat
Crimson Heat

Standalone
A Touch of Menage Boxed Set
Shades of Menage Boxed Set
Naughty Girl Desires Boxed Set
Nice Girl Naughty
Sinderella Sexy
The Biker and The Bride
The Fire Within
Bared to Him
Pleasure Bound : A Futuristic Adult Romance Boxed Set
Merry Menage Kisses Boxed Set
Inner Girl Rising
Stripped Naked
Risqué Girl Delights Boxed Set
A Holiday Menage
Ménage À Trois
A Hitman for Hannah
Billionaire Boyfriend

Edible Delights
Vampira
Toygasm
The Dark Side

Watch for more at www.janspringer.com.

After spending ten years in a maximum-security prison, Jennifer Jane (JJ) Watson got early parole and a job on a remote Canadian cattle ranch playing housekeeper to three of the sexiest cowboys she's ever met...a single woman shouldn't be experiencing such scorching ménages with three sexy-as-sin men. Her love for her cowboys continues to grow as she gives into the fevered heat and scorching passions she feels for each of them.

Passion burns bright when she's wrapped in the arms of her cowboys. But JJ's simmering restlessness explodes and she's seriously making up for lost time by pursuing her dreams. There's only one little problem. She hasn't revealed to her bosses what she's been up to while they're away tending to the cattle and doing their ranch chores. She knows when they discover her secret, there will be hell to pay.

Ranchers Rafe, Dan and Brady have found the woman who completes them. She makes their secluded ranch a home-sweet-home. She's vulnerable, sweet and willing to share her bed with all three of them. But when JJ's secret is unwittingly revealed, they're stunned, angry and they figure its time to dole out some fiery punishment in some mighty naughty ways.

Cowboys Online~Moose Ranch
Cowboys for Christmas – Book One
Cowboys In Her Pocket – Book Two
Loving Her Cowboys – Book Three
Cowboys In Her Heart – Book Four
Always Her Cowboys – Book Five

Published by Spunky Girl Publishing
Copyright 2016 by Jan Springer
Discover other titles by Jan Springer at http:www.janspringer.com
Cover art by Talina Perkins ~ Bookin' It Designs
Edited by Julie Naughton

Note

This is a work of fiction. Characters, places, settings and events presented in this book are purely of the author's imagination and bear no resemblance to any actual person, living or dead or to any actual events, places and/or settings.

Chapter One

"SOMETHING'S UP WITH JJ," Dan mumbled beneath his breath as the three of them went about packing the ATV trailers in the vehicle shed.

"She has been acting differently lately," Brady agreed.

"Happier," Rafe commented as he hitched his trailer to his machine.

"Yeah, happier." Dan agreed. That was it. She did seem more cheerful. She had been in a bit of a funk since spring when her stepbrother had come around. He had stalked her and then kidnapped her. They'd been lucky that things hadn't turned out worse than they did.

Dan shivered involuntarily as a burst of anger grabbed him. The incident had been too scary for all of them. The close call had made all three of them more protective of JJ.

Dan forced his dark thoughts of that horrible night back to the work at hand and quickly tossed his knapsack beside the two bear-proof coolers in the trailer hooked to his own ATV.

They were heading out to the mid-pastures to move more cows through the forests to the fresher northern pastures. Those meadows were closer to the railroad and when the time came in October for the final cattle drive, the cows that were ready for slaughter would be closer to transportation and ready to go.

They estimated that this particular trip that began today would last three days. It was the longest they had ever been away from JJ.

Over the past weeks of August, they had been working hard doing the haying and also moving small herds farther and farther north. But they had made it a point that at least one of them was with JJ every night. This would be Dan's last time away from her until the October cattle drive which would keep them from JJ for a week.

He was pretty nervous leaving her here on her own. They all were. Except JJ.

He had expected her anxiety and panic attacks to kick in by now, but at breakfast she had been cheerful.

"She's up to something," Rafe muttered beneath his breath as he tied a tarp over the supplies in his trailer.

"She's cute when she's up to something," Brady said with a grin.

"Hey, she's always cute," Rafe interjected.

They all laughed and agreed.

"If I didn't have to get these tags onto the cattle during this last trip, I would be having a repeat performance of last night," Dan teased them. He couldn't help but brag, just a little, after spending his night alone with JJ.

The three of them took turns with her. They each had their alone night with her and then every fourth evening they shared her. He had never met such a willing female sexual partner. It was liberating.

He suspected her exploration of sex had something to do with spending so many years in prison. She had not expected to get out ten years earlier. Had he been in her shoes, he would be catching up for lost time too.

"Well, Dan, my man, not to worry, because the first one back here in three days will have some quality time with her. And I'm betting it will be me." Brady flashed his even white teeth at Dan.

Son of a bitch.

"So that's why you picked the southeast quarter to work. It was closer to the ranch. Sneaky," Dan growled.

Lucky bastard. He wished he had thought of that.

"Let's just get our asses moving. The faster we get our work finished, the faster we get back to find out what JJ is up to," Rafe said with a wink. He placed his helmet over his head and buckled the strap.

A moment later, he fired up his vehicle, tossed the guys a wave, and roared out of the shed, leaving a blue cloud of acrid-smelling fuel.

"That little bugger. He thinks this is a race," Brady said with a shake of his head. His eyes glittered with mischief and a second later, he'd placed on his helmet, fired up his vehicle and, with a quick wave to Dan, followed Rafe.

For a moment, Dan thought about staying for a couple of hours with JJ. Just to keep her company and ask her if she really was okay with them being away from her for so long. But then he frowned at the idea. She would think he was just being a clucking mother hen. He needed to trust her when she said she would be fine.

He shoved his safety helmet onto his head, buckled it, straddled his machine and a moment later he angled his vehicle out of the shed and closed the door. He climbed back onto his vehicle and tossed a wave to JJ, who was hanging laundry on an outdoor clothesline.

She waved back and looked quite happy. A wide smile brightened her face and her long auburn hair blew in the autumn wind.

Well, hell, she didn't appear nervous at all. Yep, she was definitely up to something.

Whew, I thought the guys would never leave.

JJ breathed a sigh of relief as Dan's ATV disappeared up the trail where Rafe and Brady had just gone.

Hurriedly, she finished hanging the clothes and rushed into the ranch house to get ready.

Half an hour later, JJ stood on the dock gazing out across the choppy blue waters, watching the white bush plane as it glided toward her on the lake.

Good heavens! Her heart was about to bust right out of her chest at the thought of what she was about to do.

Had she totally lost her mind? Yes, she must have. Her legs began to shake as she spied the flight instructor's face in the window.

Kaley waved. Her pretty smile did little to alleviate JJ's anxiety. Her stomach rolled with anxiety.

Oh God, she was going to be sick. She was going to puke right here. She was going to hurl her breakfast right into the lake.

But JJ also knew, after being sick, she *would* climb into that plane. Just like she had been doing all summer, every time the guys had been away.

Exposure therapy. It was a bitch. But it worked for her. With the help of cognitive therapy — learning to change the way she talked to herself about doom and gloom scenarios of the plane's walls closing in on her — she had also been practicing how to breathe through the panic her active imagination created.

To make matters even more challenging, she'd obtained her student pilot license and had been learning how to fly a small plane. This plane was a pretty big one compared to what the other pilots at North Country Air flew, but Kaley swore it was the best. Her Cessna Caravan could hold up to sixteen passengers and a bunch of cargo. It was a 1997 and had been brought over from Sweden in 2006 by a pilot friend of Kaley's. Kaley had purchased it for way over a million dollars in 2008.

"Are you ready, JJ? We're forgoing the outside pre-flight inspection since I know you know it perfectly," Kaley called from the open doorway. Her shoulder-length wavy honey-blonde hair blew around her face in the wind. She had expertly maneuvered the Cessna right up along the side of the large dock and she was waving to JJ to come inside.

Kaley's shout snapped JJ out of her momentary funk. She grabbed her knapsack, the one she carried on her with all her emergency items; a first aid kit, water, water purifying tablets,, waterproof matches, a tiny emergency stove and dried packs of food, in case the plane had to make an emergency landing.

She tossed the pack to Kaley who caught it with ease and dropped it inside the plane.

"Now, your turn," Kaley said in a firm voice.

JJ froze as a wave of panic descended over her. Her throat went dry and her heart began a crazy fast beat.

Shit! Now was not the time to lose it.

"You can do it. Just breathe and don't forget those happy thoughts!" Kaley shouted.

JJ nodded jerkily.

Happy thoughts. Yeah, right.

Oh man, she was nuts doing this.

"Come on, JJ. Remember. Baby steps. You have been doing this all summer. Let's go or the plane will float away without you and you'll have to swim for it. You don't want to do that, do you?" Kaley flashed JJ a huge smile that popped out deep dimples in Kaley's cheeks.

She extended her hand and JJ didn't hesitate. She swallowed her panic, stepped onto the nearest pontoon and grabbed Kaley's hand.

She *could* do this. She *would* do this. She wanted so badly to be free from her fears and become an asset to her men. Being able to fly them in and out of here, especially if there was a health emergency...the helplessness of being unable to help Dan by getting him to a hospital this past spring had been the flame that had lit her wick to get her ass in gear and retrain her brain.

In a moment, she was in the plane and Kaley had placed JJ's knapsack on one of the seats nearest to the cockpit.

"Oh hey, I got some mail for you," Kaley said as she held out a letter. JJ accepted the white envelope.

Who in the world would be writing to her here? She had no friends, aside from a handful of female pilots at North Country Air who knew her. A quick glance at the name and address had JJ frowning. The letter was from a former cellmate of hers from the penitentiary.

She wished she could read the letter now, but instead she tucked it into a side pocket of her knapsack. She would have to read it later.

It was time to fly.

She sat in the pilot's seat, and checked the gauges. Everything looked good. It was textbook perfect.

Kaley did a great job in maintaining her plane, and so far JJ had never come across a problem during the in-flight checks.

"Okay, start the plane and take her down to the other end of lake just like the last time."

JJ nodded. Unfamiliar confidence whispered through her.

Yeah, she could do this. Just like last time. She had already taken the plane around the lake many times. She knew how to read the instrument panel like the back of her hand. Heck, when she was asleep, she even dreamed that she was flying.

Yes. She could do this.

JUST ONE MORE NIGHT, until I see JJ again, Brady thought as he stared into the orange flames of the evening campfire. He chuckled and shook his head. He'd realized months ago that every time he was alone, his thoughts drifted to JJ. And many times, just like now, he would remember the first time he'd seen her. She'd stepped off the small plane where it had landed on the frozen lake right outside of their ranch.

Brady had asked his sister, Jenna, to send a man or two, through her Cowboys Online business where she supplied ex-cons with jobs on ranches. But JJ had turned out to be a woman, and she had been wrapped from head to toe in winter gear, as if she'd been afraid of the cold.

She'd also been drunk, having broken into the North Country Air pilot's cargo of wine she was supposed to deliver to the wilderness retreat a hundred miles east of Moose Ranch. Turned out JJ had a claustrophobia problem, accompanied by anxiety and panic, and had hoped the wine would calm her nerves. It had, and it had made her pretty bold that night too. She had told him between hiccups that he was grumpy but cute.

Brady smiled. Truth be told though, despite his anger at his sister, Jenna, for deceiving them in sending them a woman instead of a man, JJ had been the prettiest woman he'd ever laid eyes on.

He had never imagined she could become more beautiful. But she had.

His heart hurt every time he thought about her being caged like an animal for ten years in a penitentiary. Anger pushed aside his hurt when he thought of why she had been put in prison in the first place. Something as simple as self-defense with extenuating circumstances should have gotten her probation or exonerated. Hell, her case should never have gone to trial in the first place.

Thankfully, she had eventually been given a full pardon. She could go anywhere, yet she stayed here with them.

Brady frowned. Did she stay because she couldn't get herself on a plane and fly out of here due to her anxiety? If she had no anxiety or panic issues, would she have left them? Because of her problems, did she feel like a prisoner, except with imaginary bars?

A wolf howled off in the distance and Brady shivered at the lonesome sound. He tossed another split log onto the fire. Yellow sparks burst into the black sky. The fire flared higher but did little to chase away the chill in the air.

Brady zipped up his jean jacket, hunkered into his makeshift chair and pulled his cowboy hat lower over his ears. Soon he would have to turn in this hat for a toque, because winter was coming. But by wearing his cowboy hat, he felt close to JJ.

He grinned. Her fascination with cowboy hats amused him. She said they turned her on. And boy, did they. Her eyes would sparkle and she had this cute little half-smile when she got the three of them wearing their hats at the same time.

A cow bawled from somewhere close by. Through the drifts of mist, he could make out the silhouettes of cattle as they settled for the night. The last couple of days he had moved over a hundred animals. Some to other pastures and some to this pasture. Tomorrow he would move many more dozen. Then he would go home and have his night with JJ..

Man, he could hardly wait to see her again. But in the meantime...He reached for his satellite phone.

"Hi Brady! Where are you now? Did you have supper? Are you cold?" JJ asked in a gush as she heard Brady's voice on the phone.

Static crackled and for a moment she thought the call had already been dropped but then Brady answered.

"Just sitting here by the fire freezing my ass off, baby girl. How's it going your end? Are you all right? Did the guys call you already?"

JJ grinned.

All three men had called her every night, checking up on her. She looked forward to evenings and to their conversations after flying the skies and then returning to the ranch to play the domestic woman. She was experiencing the best of both worlds. Pilot and hausfrau.

"I heard from Rafe earlier and I just got off with Dan. You didn't answer my question about supper. You weren't too tired to cook something warm, were you?"

Brady chuckled.

"You old mother hen. Yes, I had supper and I must say those chocolate eclairs you made tasted damned good my first night. If you were here, I would have made you lick the cream off my lips."

Warmth burst through her at Brady's compliment. She loved it when the guys couldn't get enough of her cooking and her baking.

"Chocolate eclairs, like in plural. You ate all three of them at once? I made one for each night. And each of them big enough so you wouldn't need to eat all three of them at once."

Laughter. "Too late."

JJ shook her head. Gosh, she ached for him to be back here with her. It was too miserable a night for them to be away and outdoors. Although Rafe and Dan had old cabins to hunker down in, Brady was in an area of the ranch tonight where there was no cabin.

A gust of wind blew against the office windows and a shiver crept up her back at the creepy noise. Ordinarily it wouldn't have bothered her, but she'd been here alone the past two nights and the loneliness of them being away was starting to get to her. How in the world would she survive it in October when they were gone for a whole week?

JJ looked out the window. It was pitch-black outside. She couldn't even see the lake. And from all that wind pummelling against the ranch house, she knew autumn was coming in like a lion. She would not be surprised in the least if the electricity went out. She glanced at the shelf by the doorway to the hall and relaxed. A flashlight stood there in case it was needed.

"Did you put your long johns on?" she asked, trying to keep her voice cheerful. Despite her uneasiness, JJ didn't want Brady picking up that anxiety was creeping around her tonight. He had a job to do and babysitting her was not one of them.

"Wish you were here with me so you could see exactly how much action my long johns are getting in a certain area. I am missing you like crazy."

JJ's breath halted in her lungs. Naughty man.

"I really miss you too, Brady." *I miss all three of you.*

She waited for an answer and cursed silently when none came.

"Brady?" Dead silence.

Shoot. The call got dropped. She hung up. She waited a minute and tried his number. Nothing.

Another blast of wind slammed against the windows making her jump. She gazed at the clock. *Nine o'clock.*

She doubted Brady would call her back tonight. He would go to bed and that's exactly what she needed to do too. She grabbed the emergency flashlight and did a routine check to make sure all the doors and windows were locked.

Although the closest neighbor was more than a hundred kilometers away, she was still unnerved by what had happened when her stepbrother had shown up and kidnapped her months ago. She had the feeling that the horrible experience was something that would take her a long time to get over.

After a quick hot shower, she made a toasty fire in the fireplace in her bedroom. The electricity still hadn't gone out, but the wind continued to hammer at the windows, so JJ lit a candle and placed the flashlight on the night table. Removing her robe, she slipped naked between her sheets and picked up the letter Kaley had given to her today.

Sadness welled up inside JJ as she tore open the letter. Many of the women she'd met in prison had been hardened over the years of incarceration, but Milena Allen still had a gentle nature, even after being in prison twelve years.

She had a similar background to JJ. No father in the picture, no siblings and a loving mother who had taken care of Milena until her mom had died of cancer when she'd been eight. Milena had had no relatives willing to take her in so she'd been tossed from foster home to foster home. Word on the rumor mill was Milena had fallen in with the wrong crowd and ended up with a maximum prison sentence for a brutal murder while she'd been high on drugs.

They'd become close friends for a year. Milena was always badgering JJ to take available correspondence courses, but due to her anxiety issues, JJ had opted to remain in familiar surroundings in her cell with her TV and had never followed Milena's advice.

Then one day Milena hadn't shown for breakfast. JJ had been devastated to learn her friend had been shipped out to another penitentiary and they had lost touch over the years. But now Milena had found her.

Her hands trembled as she read the letter.

Dear Jennifer Jane,

I hope this letter finds you well. I just heard through the grapevine that you got an early parole through the Freedom Run and Cowboys Online programs. A huge congratulations. I am so happy for you. Didn't I tell you that you got a very bad deal? That you should never have gone to prison?

Anyways, I also heard you are working on a ranch for the brother of the woman who runs Cowboys Online. I don't know if you have any pull with his sister, but you know me personally. If you can vouch for me to that lady, I would forever be in your debt. I have put my name into both programs but have not heard anything back.

I do hope we can meet again and please know I think of you often. Sending you warm hugs. Thank you in advance for any strings you can pull.

Love, Milena Allen

Warmth flooded JJ as she remembered Milena's tendency of giving warm hugs. JJ did some mental calculations and figured Milena would be around thirty-three now. Despite having had a continuing drug problem even in prison, JJ knew deep in her heart that Milena was a caring woman. Maybe if she talked to Jenna she could look into helping out Milena too?

She had talked to Jenna a few times over the past year when she called and spoke with Brady. Jenna seemed to be a kind-hearted woman. One would have to be, in order to run a company like Cowboys Online. But JJ didn't want to take advantage of the woman and her program. She also didn't want to disappoint Milena.

Reaching over, JJ grabbed the phone and was surprised to hear a dial tone. Opening her night table drawer, she pulled out her personal phone book where she kept a handful of phone numbers and then she dialed Jenna.

Chapter Two

THE ROAR OF AN INCOMING plane early the next morning had JJ rushing out of the ranch and wincing as cold air slapped across her face as she ran along the trail down toward the lake. Dawn was breaking and spooky shadows hugged the surrounding forest, making the lake appear dark and gray.

This morning, she had slept in. In all the excitement from speaking with Jenna last night about Milena and anxiety over being alone, she had completely forgotten to set her alarm.

Chowing down a quick breakfast of cereal and some orange juice, she then grabbed her flight bag and rushed outside just in time to see Kaley angling the big white plane toward the dock. The engine roared in JJ's ears as she rushed down to the dock and hopped onto the pontoon. Kaley had already opened the doorway and JJ quickly ducked beneath the wing and climbed into the plane. The interior smelled faintly of fuel and oil. It was becoming a familiar scent. A part of her routine. A part of her life.

JJ yanked the door closed and locked it. After tossing her flight bag onto a seat, she hurried to the cockpit where Kaley had already retreated and moved into the co-pilot seat.

Her flight instructor beamed happily at her as JJ entered the cockpit.

"What?" JJ asked.

She could not understand why Kaley appeared so happy. The woman rarely cracked a grin and was usually stern.

"You, is what. This is the first time I did not have to coax you into the plane. I saw you running down the trail and thought maybe you would be too preoccupied with getting here and thinking about other things and so I hoped you would simply hop onto the plane without a second thought and you did."

JJ bit her bottom lip as a jolt of nervousness rippled through her. She tensed up as she dropped into her seat.

Shit. Kaley is right.

She had spent the morning rushing around and hadn't given her anticipatory anxiety or her worry about having up a panic attack much thought. Until now.

"Now that you're here. Let's get moving. Daylight is burning. Give me a rundown of how you plan to get us up in the air."

JJ blinked. *Up in the air?*

"You are way overdue and you are more than ready. No more excuses. Tell me how you plan on getting us into the air."

Anxiety threatened to creep in but JJ managed to chase some of the nervousness away. But just barely.

For the next few minutes, she gave Kaley a verbal checklist of the instructions she had learned. Although she had passed the theoretical tests with flying colors and done almost perfectly on the online simulator tests her flight instructor had told her to take, she still had not mastered much confidence of even getting a plane into the air, except in her dreams.

"Perfect. Now, start the engine and let's get this baby skybound."

JJ's heart quickened its pace as she gazed out the side window. The brisk breeze had pushed the plane away from the dock and they were now about half a mile from the ranch. Winds buffeted the metal sides of the plane and foot-high waves crashed into the pontoons.

Anxiety gripped JJ.

Water surrounded her. She was trapped.

She rolled her tight shoulders and blew out a tense breath.

No escape. No stepping onto solid ground. No use in panicking. Freaking out would just make her feel uneasy and screw her plans of getting her head wrapped around this project. She wanted so badly to surprise the guys with her secret.

Despite trying to talk herself into being calm, the familiar inner nervousness began to spread its ugly wings. She rolled her stiff shoulders again and focused on the gauges. Everything appeared normal.

Kaley must have picked up on her nervousness, because she suddenly reached out and placed her hand on JJ's wrist.

"Just remember, sweetie, baby steps. No task is unachievable as long as you stick to baby steps. You fall and you get right back up. Right?" Kaley's question came in a firm voice that suddenly anchored JJ.

Her flight instructor was back to business mode and for a brief second, JJ felt disoriented.

The windows seemed to waver and close in on her.

Relax. I can do this. I have come so far. Man, she really had!

JJ took several slow, deep breaths and began to feel better. She'd been practicing on steadying her breathing over the past weeks. Working on it a lot. She had been training her body and her brain on how to react when she hit the panic wall, and she was hitting it now.

JJ trembled.

Early-morning sunshine glared across the windshield, catching her attention. She smiled at the rosy glow. Suddenly she didn't feel so alone and off-balance. She had Kaley to guide her and she had the sun's friendship.

She rotated her shoulders again, finally feeling them loosen. Then she got the engine started. It roared in her ears, drowning the rapid pound of her heartbeat.

Concentrate.

JJ checked everything that needed checking. Everything looked good. She logged their departure time in the logbook and then tucked it away in the hanger beneath the seat.

She liked Kaley's plane. It was older and much bigger than the other float planes that dropped off supplies to the ranch. It kind of felt like a second home now. Yeah, right.

Quit stalling. Move.

JJ angled the plane toward the closest end of the lake and watched the sun pop up above the dark treeline. Bright sunshine blasted across the white-capped waves. When she reached close to the end of the lake, she turned the plane around.

Confidence soared. She moved the plane forward. This part was all second nature to her. Familiar. Comforting.

She increased the speed. The pontoons slapped noisily against the waters.

"Increase your power. Gently," Kaley said softly.

JJ's mouth went dry as the other end of the lake quickly came into sight. Her heart crashed against her chest as she did as Kaley instructed and increased power. The roar of the engines grew louder. She followed what she'd learned in the flight simulator and within seconds the plane felt lighter as it lifted off the waves and moved into the air.

Oh, sweet heavens! I am freaking flying!

For a moment, her mind blanked. Now what? She couldn't think. Couldn't remember. This was all so overwhelming. She was flying!

Thankfully, Kaley gave her the next instruction and JJ suddenly remembered what to do. She angled the plane higher and moments later they soared over the pine trees that hugged the rocky shoreline of the lake.

Euphoria snapped through JJ as she gazed down. She gasped at the beauty of the green forests, the black waters of the creeks, the winding blue rivers and the patchwork of sparkling meadows.

"What are those black and brown dots?" JJ asked as she pointed to one particular meadow.

"Those are your cattle down there," Kaley commented.

She wished she could search for the guys but she focused her attention ahead.

Pristine blue skies loomed. She felt weightless. She was free.

She was crazy.

"You did it! Well done!" Kaley cheered. "Keep at this altitude and let's take a ride."

For the next hour, JJ followed Kaley's instructions on where to fly. They flew over massive forested areas dotted with blue lakes. Occasional blasts of wind buffeted the plane, but JJ managed to compensate.

"Want to take the plane down?" Kaley asked as the lake with the ranch finally zoomed into view.

For a moment, JJ wanted to say no. She had never landed the plane before. But then an inner voice urged her to try because before today, she had never flown a plane, either.

Momentary euphoria grabbed hold, making JJ giddy. Then reality crashed in around her. She had a plane to land!

She swallowed and nodded jerkily. Shivers raced through her and her hands tightened around the wheel. Her shoulders tensed. She hadn't realized she'd been holding the wheel so tightly until her shoulders began to ache. She lined up the plane with the center of the lake and began her descent.

After a couple of instructions from Kaley, JJ exhaled as the pontoons hit the water with a massive splash. She barely heard Kaley cheer as JJ slowly turned the plane toward the dock about a quarter of a mile away.

"Okay, let's trade places and I will dock us. You look beat," Kaley said as she stood.

She was more than beat. She was exhausted.

Her legs shook like mad as they exchanged seats. Disbelief rushed over her as she stared out the window and watched the dock and ranch come closer.

Oh dear Lord. She had actually done it. She had flown and landed a freaking plane.

And you thought you couldn't do it, a cynical voice chided her from deep inside.

Well, it seemed she would not be able to use that excuse anymore. She could do things, despite her uncomfortable anxiety and panic disorder.

Yes, she could.

"I've heard about your delicious brownies from Blue and Kelly. These brownies are why I wanted to be your flight instructor," Kaley commented as JJ set a plate full of brownies on top of the coffee table beside the coffeepot and mugs she'd brought out earlier.

"And here I thought it was because you loved the challenge of getting a panic and anxiety induced woman into the air?" JJ chuckled and then she remembered something.

"Hold on. I have got a little surprise for you," JJ said.

She rushed back into the kitchen and reached into a high cupboard where she had tucked something away. Way in back, she grabbed a small gift-wrapped package. Her hands shook and she almost dropped it.

Since stepping off the plane, JJ had not been able to stop trembling. It wasn't from her anxiety, but everything to do with her excitement at actually accomplishing one of her newfound dreams. Learning to fly.

The sense of achievement just about drove her crazy. She wanted to shout her news through the forest. She wanted to tell the guys...

JJ sobered. Until now, she hadn't told them a thing. She'd gone behind their backs and a sudden burst of guilt nibbled away at her newfound confidence. How would she break the news to the guys? Oh heck, she would think about that later. Right now, she had something for Kaley.

"Kaley, this is for you," JJ said as she settled down on the couch beside Kaley and handed her the gift which she'd wrapped in a pretty lilac-colored paper with matching bow. Surprise washed over the flight instructor's face and she set her half-eaten brownie down on her plate. She clutched her hands to her chest and shook her head. Surprise etched her blue eyes.

"JJ, you shouldn't have. This is so sweet of you."

"Come on, open it. I hope you like it."

A rare smile lifted Kaley's lips and JJ was glad she'd decided on getting her a present.

"When I saw it, I thought of you. I remember you said you came from the East Coast not too far from Boston and you had once mentioned that you used to go sailing with a couple of guys who were brothers."

A wistful expression whispered across the woman's face. For a moment, she frowned and JJ had the feeling she might have made a mistake. But when Kaley gingerly removed the bow and carefully ripped open the paper, opened the small black velvet box and pulled out a delicate silver necklace with a cute little sailboat, her mouth dropped open with shock. Tears sparkled in her eyes.

"This is just gorgeous, JJ," she whispered. "Would you put it on me? I'm great flying the plane, but I am lousy with delicate jewelry." She held up her two hands and wiggled her scarred fingers.

JJ had noticed the scars lacing Kaley's fingers and arms, but she had never pried about what had happened to her.

Happiness blew away JJ's fear of having made a mistake and moments later Kaley was all smiles as she wore the necklace, sipped her coffee and popped a second brownie into her mouth. She made some funny appreciative sounds and as she chewed her eyes widened and she shook her head.

"These are utterly unbelievably delicious," Kaley said after she swallowed.

Pride made JJ urge Kaley to take another brownie.

"These will go straight to my hips. But well worth it. JJ can I get the recipe sometime?"

"Sure, I'll email it to you. It's actually a recipe that I made up on my own for the guys. It involves beer. But don't worry you won't get drunk."

Kaley laughed. "Beer? No way."

"It's true. The guys love them."

Kaley's expression went to one of extreme excitement. "I bet they do. You should go into business and sell these."

"Yeah, and deliver them by plane," JJ added, not really taking Kaley seriously.

"I could imagine all those hermits and ranchers living in solitude waiting for your baked goods, JJ. It would really make their day. But you need to get your license first."

Hmm, that was an interesting idea, but she was just a newbie. It took time to learn how to bake professionally and she just had too much to do right here on the ranch.

"Hey let's not get ahead of ourselves. I'm just starting out flying, and besides, I don't even have a plane," JJ said with a chuckle. Kaley was just being silly. Wasn't she?

"I can keep an eye out for a used one when one comes up for sale. You can grab a loan from one of the banks or secure a personal loan from someone."

JJ shrugged her shoulders.

When JJ didn't answer, Kaley's hand hovered over the mound of brownies.

"I just cannot get enough. May I have another one?"

"Please, eat as many as you like. I'll make up a doggie bag and you can take them home. They freeze really well."

"All. I want them all but I couldn't ask that. I would be too greedy. But a doggie bag would be so sweet of you. I realize you need to feed your cowboys."

"Seriously, Kaley, you are the one who is sweet. Taking me on, knowing all the challenges I have just getting on a plane."

"Girlfriend, believe you me. I know challenges."

Kaley held up her hands.

"Do you see these? They were so burned I was told I probably would never be able to use them and I would be lucky if I didn't lose all of these." She wiggled her fingers. "I got lucky."

"I don't mean to pry, but how did you burn your hands and arms?"

Kaley shook her head and bit her bottom lip.

"Now there's a story. A car accident during a snowstorm. I was burned all over my body, actually. My face too. I was with my two men friends, the ones with the sailboat. We skidded off the road. I was the only one wearing a seat belt. They were thrown from the car and injured badly but I was caught in the car and couldn't get the seatbelt off. I was unconscious when the car caught fire. The emergency personnel couldn't get me out in time, so I was burning alive." Kaley shivered and JJ wished she hadn't asked the question in the first place.

"I was able to get plastic surgery for my face but the rest of me...well, let's say, over the years, it's been a work in progress. I have only a couple more surgeries and I should be as good as new."

"Wow, I had no idea," JJ replied.

"I don't advertise my history. But rest assured pretty much most of the ladies who fly for North Country Air have had challenges. So, we understand what you were up against."

"Were up against? I don't think I am out of the woods yet."

"Consider yourself a work in progress then. You will know when you have healed enough to really live again. Speaking of living...those three sexy bosses of yours. When are you going to tell them about your flying lessons? And why keep it a secret in the first place?" Kaley asked. Curiosity shone in her eyes as she perched at the edge of her seat, totally excited.

"I mean, keeping such a secret from your bosses. Won't that give them trust issues or something? I mean with the four of you living here...okay, sorry. I should just mind my own business."

JJ shook her head.

"No it's fine. You shared personal stuff with me, so I should do the same. I didn't tell them because I didn't want them talking me out of it."

Kaley frowned. "You don't think they would support you in your decision?"

"They would worry too much. Flying planes is dangerous, they'd say."

"Well, it's true. It can be at times. But, it's no different than any other vehicle. Just keep the time logs accurate so you know when the plane needs to have its regular checkup. Do your preflight inspections and look out for and listen for anything unusual. Keep an eye on the weather and don't take any risks upon landing in areas you don't know...unless of course it's an emergency landing."

Kaley stopped and laughed.

"I don't know why I am telling you all this. You know it all by heart. You're one of the best students I have ever had."

Wow. What a compliment!

"You said they were coming back tomorrow night?" Kaley asked.

"Actually, I'm expecting Brady back tonight. Rafe and Dan will be in sometime tomorrow. I will have to find out when they're going away again before we schedule for flights. I will e-mail you and we can set up more lessons."

"Great. Then, we'll leave it at that."

Kaley checked her watch and frowned.

"Oh, I hadn't realized how late it's gotten. I am going to have to head back. I have another student later this afternoon. She wants to practice some night flying. How about that doggie bag of the brownies and then I will get out of your hair."

They both rose and JJ grabbed the plate of baked goods. Fifteen minutes later, she stood on the dock and waved to Kaley, who, with her bag full of sweets in hand, happily stepped into her float plane where it had been moored.

That familiar giddiness of disbelief rushed through JJ, as minutes later, she watched the white plane soar into the bright blue sky. Soon the plane disappeared over the nearby treetops. The roar of the engine turned into a purr and then the sounds of the forest took over.

A soft wind whispered through the pine boughs of the trees behind her. A woodpecker knocked on a tree and waves slapped against the rocky shoreline and dock.

JJ hugged herself and headed back up the trail toward the ranch house. There was still some housework to be done, dinner to get started and maybe a bit more studying before Brady returned.

She blew out an aroused breath as she thought about the scorching sex she would be getting when her men came home. Each of them were exceptionally eager to pleasure her after being away from her. She, too, was eager to find pleasure in their arms. She could hardly wait for them to come home.

That thought totally disintegrated as she opened the mudroom door and discovered Brady propped against the doorway to the hallway. He glowered at her. His cheeks were red. He looked pissed.

Oh shit. Had he been here all this time? Had he heard the conversation she'd had with Kaley about the plane?

"Brady. I didn't know you were back."

She struggled to control the sudden tremble in her voice as she stepped into the mudroom. She would have pushed past him, but it appeared he was in no mood to budge.

"That is apparent," he growled.

Yes, he was most definitely angry. She fought back her panic as her tummy revolted in an unusual nervousness. Guilt slammed into her hard and fast.

"It's almost suppertime. I've got leftovers for us tonight. Steak on kaisers along with beet salad and some homemade leek soup. Sounds good, doesn't it?"

She needed to act casual. Maybe he hadn't overheard? Maybe he'd just gotten in when she'd been saying goodbye to Kaley down by the dock?

Brady's frown deepened. Thankfully, he straightened from the doorframe and moved aside to allow her to pass. She brushed past quickly, avoiding eye contact. She could feel tension zip through the air and rope around her like a lasso.

"How about you run out to the garden and a grab us a head of lettuce, a couple of tomatoes and a cucumber, and I will make us a delicious salad too."

"How about you tell me what the hell is going on?" Brady growled as he followed her into the kitchen. She could feel him right behind her as she opened the fridge to grab the container with meat. Despite the cold air blowing out against her, she felt ultra warm knowing his body was inches away.

"W-what do you mean?" JJ asked as she placed the Tupperware container onto the counter. She figured it would be best to play stupid and find out exactly when he had stepped into listening in on their conversation.

"What is going on with North Country Air being here?"

Relief rushed through her.

"Is that what got you upset? Kaley dropped in for a visit. She heard about my beer brownies and I..."

In a sudden movement that took JJ by complete surprise, Brady grabbed her by her elbow and spun her around to face him.

His eyes were narrow and concern etched his face.

"Why are you lying to me, JJ?"

Irritation snapped through her.

"Maybe it's none of your business, Brady."

"I'm making it my business, Jennifer Jane."

Wow. He had not called her by her real name since, well, she couldn't remember. He truly was serious.

"Brady. I am old enough to have friends visit. I hope you are not upset with that."

"I don't care if you have friends over. What I am upset with is *the flying planes is dangerous* comment, and all the rest I heard."

Darn it. He *had* been listening. JJ's shoulders sagged in defeat and to her horror, her cheeks went red-hot.

"How much exactly did you hear?"

"Pretty much everything. I came back earlier. I figured you were out for your afternoon walk so I took my gear into my room, lay down on the bed and fell asleep. Woke up to hearing voices. Came into the hall—"

JJ held out her hand to silence him.

"I didn't tell you guys because I didn't want you to worry."

"Shit, woman. Worry is an understatement. Flying *is* dangerous. Ever hear of Amelia Earhart? She was a professional and look what happened to her."

"I've been studying my ass off, Brady. I want this." She was surprised at how firm and confident her voice sounded.

His eyes softened and for a moment she thought he understood. But then, he shook his head.

"No, JJ. I won't allow it."

Surprise roared through her.

"Excuse me? You won't allow it?" Disbelief spun through her as she watched him walk to the coffee machine.

"No flying planes, JJ. End of discussion." His voice sounded dark and final as he prepared the coffee.

Was this guy for real?

"You don't have a say, Brady."

"As long as you are living here, I have a say. As long as you are my woman, I have a say. As long as you allow me to make love to you, I have a say."

My woman? Make love to you? Not have sex, but make love? Excitement made JJ's chest tighten.

He turned back around. He appeared frustrated as he rubbed his hand over his five o'clock shadow.

"Brady..." She wanted to argue with him. To pound into his head that he could not control what she wanted to do with her life.

"I know I don't have the right to boss you around, JJ. I know I don't. Hell, I don't want to argue. I kept thinking about you when I was gone. You look so beautiful. I missed you like crazy." The deep chorus of his voice stroked like silk over her senses. The fuck-me-now look in his eyes had her thighs clenching and her vagina throbbing with need.

All her thoughts of arguing with him disintegrated as his firm hands circled her waist like a scorching brand. He lifted her off her feet, took several steps and then promptly placed her ass onto the kitchen countertop. She slapped her hands onto the counter to steady herself and whimpered at the need flaring in his eyes.

In a flash, Brady's hands flew to the top button on her blouse. His breaths came fast and harsh as he unbuttoned.

"No arguments," he whispered. "I just want you, baby."

His male scent dominated her and she felt helpless as he pushed the material of her blouse aside, then he studied her bra-covered breasts. Intense heat whipped through her at his hungry expression. He dipped his fingers beneath the straps and slowly slid them down her shoulders and past her elbows, allowing her breasts to spill free of the lacy cups. He cupped her and she cried out as he dipped his head. His mouth latched onto her right nipple. Blistering heat and erotic pressure made her shudder.

Brady sucked and nibbled and licked. Her nipple throbbed as he moved on to her other one. JJ wished she could formulate thoughts, but nothing came to mind. Just pure pleasure and excitement.

His lips were red and so were her nipples when moments later he lifted his head. Her bare belly quivered when his fingers touched her flesh as he slipped his fingers beneath the waistband of her track pants. Within seconds, her pants and panties were removed.

Brady dropped to his knees before her and instinctively she widened her legs. His lust-drenched expression sent want zipping along her every nerve. Awareness had her watching his every move with wicked anticipation.

JJ moaned softly as his face moved closer. The tip of his tongue slipped past his parted lips and she trembled as his mouth fused over her clitoris. His tongue dashed over and around her clit, tracing sensual patterns, rocking pleasure deep into her belly and between her thighs.

His mouth moved faster. His lips sucked on her labia, his teeth gently nipped her flesh and his tongue laved her. Her legs melted and quivered beneath sensations. Soon she was keening and struggling to kick her feet up in an effort to wrap them around his head, but her legs were too pleasure heavy. Her lungs shuddered as she breathed. She tried to lift her hands off the counter, but she stopped, realizing if she did, she would end up falling backward.

Desperation clutched her.

"Brady, take me now," she breathed harshly.

He kept eating her pussy as if not hearing.

"Brady, I need you... please," she hissed.

Suddenly, he was standing. He was still fully clothed! She moaned in frustration.

JJ's eyelids were so heavy she could barely see him as his hands flew to his belt buckle. A moment later, Brady unzipped his jeans. He growled as he struggled to push his pants and underwear past his hips.

Then he moved in front of her, grabbed a condom package from his shirt pocket, and seconds later he had himself fully sheathed.

Despite how intense things got between them, Brady was always well prepared when it came to protection. All three men were. It allowed JJ to be carefree and to really enjoy sex without having to think about guarding herself.

She had expected some foreplay. Erotic kisses, a little more tender touches. But he gripped her by her hips, and pulled her close to the edge of the counter. She shuddered and gasped as he pressed his big cock into her sensitized vagina. Enormous pressure took her breath away. She could feel his entire length of his flesh throb hot and hard inside her. In an instant he withdrew, she gasped when he drove into her again.

Quickly, he began a steady rhythm that had her once again feeling helpless as pleasure crashed toward her.

Muscles constricted everywhere. She scrunched her hands into fists and clenched her jaw. Sparkling stars burst behind her closed eyes. Her thighs tightened. JJ's pussy muscles shuddered. She moaned at his every thrust. Loved how hard and fast he pistoned.

Her senses were exploding and her body became his as he fully controlled her with his shaft.

"Who do you belong to, baby?" Brady growled. His deep voice encouraged her to submit.

"You," she hissed.

Brady pumped faster.

"You are *mine*, JJ." His voice was a caress.

He thrust harder, deeper. The friction of his pubic bone rubbing against her clit snapped waves of pleasure through her and his rapid strokes plunged her into climax.

Shudders rocked her. JJ gasped as she fought for air. She bucked against his fiery force. Her breasts swayed and bounced with his every thrust. Tremors shook her. The sensations were shockingly beautiful as she became lost in the seductive world.

Brady took her hard. Over and over. He was angry with her. Pissed that she had kept something so important like her flying a plane hidden from them.

He pistoned deeper. Groaned and gritted his teeth as the heavy length of his cock was embraced by her tight, warm welcoming muscles. Her lips were parted and sweet little gasps escaped her pretty mouth. Her eyes were closed. Her bare breasts jiggled and her nipples were red from his sucking.

The harder he took her, the louder her moans. JJ's sensual sounds caressed his senses, making him thrust faster, bringing him closer to the pleasure he craved.

She had no right to put her life in danger.

Damn her!

Man, she was so beautiful. So loving. He couldn't bear something happening to her. Whenever he was near her, he couldn't stop looking at her. Even now, as he made love to her, he wanted to keep his eyes open and watch the pleasure splash over her flushed face.

Heat and pressure curled around his rigid shaft as her sweet, warm muscles clenched him.

She had stolen his heart the minute he had seen her. He moaned as his entire body tightened. Shudders swept through him like dynamite. His anger vanished and Brady gave into the exploding waves of pleasure.

Chapter Three

RAFE HUNCHED DEEPER into his jacket as the cold wind bit into his face. Darkness was descending fast and the headlights on his machine didn't give him the illumination he required at this speed. But he didn't want to slow down. He was cold and hungry and shelter was just up ahead.

Angling his ATV around a huge pothole, he wrenched the wheel and swerved to avoid a head-sized rock that had rolled down an embankment onto the trail. Man, that had been close.

Any given day, while out on the trails, Rafe encountered one thing or another. Either a tree had fallen onto the trail or deep trenches had been carved into a makeshift road by heavy rainfall.

Yesterday, he had almost hit a giant moose who'd decided to take an afternoon nap right at the entrance of one of the meadows were he had been traveling to. Thankfully, he'd seen the big dark animal with huge antlers just in time to allow him to come to an abrupt halt.

Hopefully, no more close calls. Tonight was his last night away from JJ. He only had a few dozen more cattle to move tomorrow and then he would head back home. It was a good thing they had laid out all the necessary fencing along each trail between the meadows, as it made the moving of the cattle so much easier and faster.

Rafe frowned as he remembered that he had found a couple of carcasses in one of the meadows. The two cows had been taken down by a pack of hungry wolves. Cattle kills happened. It was a hazard of raising Angus in an organic, unprotected setting.

If the pack became too much of a problem, some tracking would be needed to find the wolves and take them down with the rifle. But this particular kill had happened weeks ago and the wolves appeared to have left the area.

His stomach rumbled and Rafe sighed with relief when he spotted the silhouette of the old shack he had been heading for. The small shelter had been built many years ago by the lumber barons who had clear-cut through this area. Now the building was used for their ranch.

Rafe parked his vehicle, slung the knapsack on his back, grabbed his rifle and the cooler from the trailer, stomped up the steps, crossed the porch and headed into the unlocked structure. Damp, cold air greeted him and he shivered, wishing he was at home with a roaring fire in the living room fireplace, playing cards with Dan and Brady and catching glimpses of JJ as she washed the dishes or made them coffee.

Damn, he missed her like crazy. She was their backbone. She took care of them. She cooked up a storm, kept the ranch house clean and boy, she was good in bed. He just didn't know what good shit he'd done in his life to deserve such a beautiful woman.

He tossed the rifle, cooler and knapsack onto the rustic table, grabbed some matches from the waterproof container they kept in each of the buildings on the property, opened the door to the woodstove and struck the match.

The small yellow flame allowed him to see the pieces of newspaper and birch bark sticking out from between the dry kindling and split logs that had been placed inside the stove by whomever of the three of them had last been here.

They always made sure before leaving one of the dozen sheds or cabins on the property that the wood stove was always filled with wood and ready for use. Rafe smiled as the pine kindling crackled and burst into flames.

Quickly, he slammed the door shut and adjusted the flue in order to allow more air into the stove so the wood would burn faster. Within a minute, heat breezed against Rafe's face and he rubbed his cold hands until they warmed.

Then he stood and grabbed a cast-iron frying pan from one of the cupboards, placed the pan on top of the stove, and headed back to his gear on the table. From the cooler, he grabbed the large Tupperware container with the words *Rafe Sunday supper* written on the masking tape. He liked JJ's feminine writing. It was free and easygoing, just like her.

From the container he grabbed a foil-wrapped item and discovered it contained a slab of pre-cooked salted bear meat. He cut the meat into thin slices and placed them into the pan. The meat sizzled and the sound made his mouth water.

He also found some margarine along with three eggs. He dropped the margarine into the pan, and when it was melted, he cracked the eggs and added them. His mouth watered as he watched his meal bubble beneath the heat.

A few minutes later, he sat at the table amidst a couple of lit short, white candles and enjoyed his meal. When he was finished, he sipped on the ice-cold beer he had retrieved from his knapsack and allowed his mind to drift through what work was left for tomorrow.

Upon inspecting the perimeter of one of the meadows, he'd noticed part of the fence had been pulled down by a fallen tree. The tree needed to be cut and that fence needed to be repaired before he could move the cattle into the area. Afterward, he would get the cattle secured and then he would head for home.

He leaned back in his chair and gazed around the cabin. One wall was lined with bunkbeds that could house up to a dozen lumberjacks. The crude beds looked uncomfortable, tossed together with rough-hewn pine planks.

Rafe carried a small, portable air mattress with his gear. He liked to think of the mattress as his home away from home bed comfort. But the air mattress was nothing compared to the comfortable ones back at the ranch.

Thinking about the cozy ranch house they had carved into the forest, loneliness sifted through Rafe. He tried to concentrate on polishing off his beer, but the isolation of the bunkhouse had him standing.

It had gotten too hot inside, compliments of the woodstove. Time for some fresh air. He grabbed his bottle and headed outdoors. Where the cold had not been welcome a short time earlier, it relieved the heat now as he stepped outside.

A brisk, refreshing wind whipped against him making him catch his breath. In the sky, he spied mysterious ribbons of green light and he smiled. The northern lights would keep him company tonight.

Rafe leaned his elbows against the wood railing of the porch, and sipped his beer. The liquid washed a cold passage down his throat. Somewhere, not too far off, a wolf howled. The eerie sound sliced through the quiet and sent creepy ripples up and down his spine. A moment later, came an answering cry.

Not too long after, he spied two gray wolves saunter past the cabin. He toyed with the idea of going inside and grabbing his rifle. But decided against it. He was not about to shoot a couple of wolves unless he knew they were the ones that had taken down those cows.

When the animals disappeared into the darkness of the nearby forest, Rafe gazed back up at the northern lights again and felt lonelier than ever.

Man, he missed JJ like crazy.

"You what?" Dan shouted as he and Brady sat at the dining room table the next afternoon. Dan stared at JJ in disbelief after what she had just revealed to him.

Brady gave her an "I told you so" look that should have irritated her, but she was too tired to be mad, because Brady had kept her up most of the night making love to her. They had slept in until the roar of Dan's vehicle had woken them this afternoon.

Brady had hopped into the shower and JJ had rushed off to make the two men a hearty lunch of fresh salad from the garden along with steamed potatoes and canned tuna.

"I'm learning to fly a plane. I've been taking lessons when you guys have been gone. Yesterday, I flew the plane for the very first time."

Dan's mouth dropped open. He stared at her with a surprised look.

Out of all three, Dan was the most humorous and laid back, yet when it came to her well-being, he was just as overprotective as the other two.

"Earth to Dan. Did you hear what JJ said?" Brady chuckled as he waved a hand in front of Dan's face. Finally, he blinked. Confusion rocked his features.

"I'm sorry, but did I hear you just say you're going for a pilot's license?"

JJ nodded. She came around and poured more coffee into his mug.

"Kaley is keeping her eyes open for a used plane similar to the one she has. One that we can interchange to use in the winter with skis so we can land on the frozen lake, as well as pontoons for spring, summer and autumn landing on water and also with wheels to land at airports."

Dan gazed over at Brady and frowned.

"She is kidding, right? I mean panic attacks, anxiety issues, plus claustrophobia and planes don't mix."

"Exposure therapy. Baby steps. Cognitive therapy." JJ said.

Dan's frown deepened.

"Cognitive therapy. I've heard of that. They say it can work."

"Yes it can. It takes time. I'm learning how to think and react a different way to certain situations. Kaley, over at North Country Air, is teaching me cognitive therapy. She's a licensed flight instructor. Kelly and Blue introduced me to her. Kaley studied at one time to be a psychologist, so she knows some stuff about anxiety. She's been helping me with my anxiety and teaching me how to fly. She has thousands of hours of flying experience. They say she's one of the best flight instructors in Northern Ontario."

Confusion continued to mar Dan's features.

"JJ has been going behind our backs all summer," Brady growled. The angry bark in his voice was back. Suddenly a light flared in Dan's eyes.

"So that's why you have been so happy lately. Freedom," Dan said.

Brady crossed his arms over his chest and nodded.

"Yeah, Rafe is the one who first mentioned she seemed happier," Brady replied.

"And here I thought it was because JJ liked living here." Dan continued to frown.

Oh shoot. Were they afraid she would leave them? Were they that insecure about her?

"If I bought a plane, it would do the business good," JJ said softly as ideas she'd been playing with tumbled out of her.

Both Dan and Brady straightened in their chairs, seemingly interested at what she had to say. Aha, an interesting reaction.

"Kaley told me that North Country Air has a new owner. Transportation and delivery prices are going to be doubled."

Dan and Brady swore.

"That's going to cut a good chunk into our profit," Dan pointed out.

"I realize that you can write transportation and delivery expenses off for taxes. With our own plane we can control those costs for one. But there are other benefits," JJ said.

"Such as?" Brady pushed. His eyes flashed with excitement.

"On a lot of occasions, it takes you guys half a day just to travel to your destination. With a float plane I can get you in and out with supplies and ATV within an hour or two. There are plenty of lakes scattered throughout your property where I can land. In winter, we interchange with skis. Of course, during times when the lakes are not frozen over you can still use the skidoos. What? Why are you both smiling?"

"Keep going. Let's hear what else you have to say," Dan urged.

JJ tried to read Brady's facial expression, but he said nothing as he continued to smile.

"Aside from the plane being beneficial with taxes, owning a plane can be more cost-effective. I can run errands to pick up and transport supplies from the city. Thunder Bay and other cities and towns have municipal airports. Rental cars and trucks at the airports are easily accessible. You use them anyway when you go to the city. We'd just need a little landing strip somewhere around here so I can use the wheels on the plane for those occasions."

"Are you saying that you would go into the city to pick up the supplies instead of relying on North Country Air? What if you have a panic attack or your anxiety kicks in and we need an order fast?" Brady asked.

JJ noticed his voice had taken on a businesslike edge. It meant he was taking her seriously.

"We could use North Country Air for emergency purposes only," Dan suggested.

Brady shook his head and JJ's hopes plummeted.

"She makes a hell of a good case," Brady said.

"But?" Dan asked.

"Flying is just too damned dangerous," Brady replied.

"There is that," Dan acknowledged with a nod.

"And I am not willing to put her life on the line just to save a few bucks," Brady muttered.

He stood and glared at JJ. She could tell he was expecting her to argue. She didn't. She would simply wait him out. Brady would cool off and then she could broach the subject again another day.

JJ was grateful when Dan remained silent, but she had a feeling she had already won him over. One down. Two more to go.

"SUPPER WAS FANTASTIC as always, JJ," Brady said as he patted his belly and smiled at JJ. Warmth coursed through her at his compliment. Since the conversation between the three of them earlier in the day, Brady and Dan had gone on with their chores as usual. Neither had brought up the subject that she had actually flown a plane.

She *had* actually flown a damned plane!

For a brief time it had been one of the happiest feelings of accomplishment she had ever experienced, until the guys had brought her crashing back to reality. Maybe she was not going to be reliable? Especially because of her anxiety issues, which unfortunately were starting to kick in.

Rafe was overdue, and she was getting the feeling something was wrong. The area of the property where Rafe had been working was the farthest from the ranch. But careful time estimates had him returning at the latest by 3:00, even if he'd gotten a late start. It was now 6:30, dark outside, cold and windy with rain in the forecast by morning.

"Earth to JJ," Brady whispered. She hadn't even seen Brady stand and stop in front of her, she'd been so deep in her worry.

"Hey, baby, Rafe will be back. It's not the first time he's been late. He could have run into a mechanical issue. Or maybe found out that more work was needed to be done with the cattle."

"Or maybe he got sick. Or hurt. Have you been able to reach him on the sat phone?" she asked.

Earlier this spring, after Dan had been injured, the guys had invested in a satellite phone system. But there were dead zones on the property, especially in the meadows surrounded by large hills. Calls got dropped continuously too. But it was better than nothing.

"No answer, but that doesn't mean anything," Dan quickly reassured.

"If he was going to stay out for another night, he would have found an area where his phone worked and sent us a message. He wouldn't keep us worrying. I know he wouldn't. Not unless something bad happened," JJ stated firmly.

She noticed the "she has a point" look that passed between both men.

Her anxiety increased. Oh why wasn't there a magic potion or some sort of exposure therapy to help her react differently when it came to worrying about her guys?

"It's quite a big area to search by ATV," Dan said.

"He could be anywhere in that quarter." Brady didn't sound hopeful.

"A search plane up in the air at first light would give us a good view," JJ burst in. She was not going to allow herself to lose hope. She just knew Rafe had run into some sort of trouble and the sooner they found him, the better.

Brady suddenly stood.

"Call North Country Air and ask them for a plane and also call the emergency people over at the Ministry," he ordered to Dan.

"I'm on it. While I'm doing that, I'll get the maps out too. We'll head out on the machines tonight before the rain starts and check if he's been at any of the shelters in the area. I think there are three of them."

Brady nodded.

"I'll get the food together," he said.

"Okay," Dan replied and he headed down the hall to the ranch office.

"I'm coming with you," JJ said as she grabbed a jar of peanut butter from a cupboard.

"No, someone needs to stay here and coordinate the rescue. You're not familiar with nighttime ATVing on the trails. Dan and I can cover more area if we split up. If I take you instead of him, it will just take longer, 'cause I'll be worrying about you." Brady said.

"I've handled the machines pretty good in daylight the few times I went out with you guys, Brady. I can do all right at night," she insisted as she began spreading peanut butter on the homemade buns she'd made this afternoon. Deep at the back of her mind, she knew he was right though.

"We're wasting time arguing," Brady grumbled. He reached into the fridge and brought out the jar of strawberry jam for her. Within seconds, he was brewing up coffee and grabbing several Thermos bottles.

JJ had a bad feeling it was going to be a long night fraught with worry.

RAFE SHIVERED AS CHILLS raged through him. He lay on the floor just inside the front door of the quickly cooling cabin. Black dots danced in front of his eyes, and as the day had gone on, Rafe had grown weaker. Early this morning he'd gone out to grab firewood from the lean to and noticed the emergency firewood running low. He'd grabbed the ax from inside the cabin and come back outside to chop some of the logs. He'd almost chopped enough wood for whomever would be using the cabin next, when in mid-swing, a loud howl from close by had startled him. In turn he'd hit the edge of the log. The ax had ricocheted, the blade bounced downward and cut deep into his shin.

The searing pain had been instant, brutal and disabling. He'd fallen over, hit the ground so hard and so carelessly that his head snapped against the edge of the cabin. Stars and pain had burst behind his eyes.

He'd been barely able to keep himself conscious to assess he was losing too much blood from his leg wound. His strength waned quickly. With shaking hands, he'd managed to undo his belt and used it as a tourniquet, securing it right above the ugly-looking gash. Then everything had gone black.

Rafe had no idea how long he'd been unconscious. Long enough, because when he'd awoken the sun was high in the sky and two gray wolves were standing a few feet away. Their gleaming white fangs were bared as they growled at him. They stood between him and the ATV where he had stupidly left his satellite phone.

He'd expected the wolves to tear into him as he crawled around to the front of the cabin. They hadn't. But they'd sniffed the air with their black noses and followed close behind him. He knew they smelled his blood. Knew if he stayed out here much longer, he would become their dinner.

With a surge of adrenaline, he managed to drag himself up the cabin stairs. Getting the door open had been a challenge. He'd grown lightheaded and passed out several times just trying to reach the doorknob. Every time he awoke, he was greeted to a pounding headache, pain searing his right leg, and surprised the wolves had not already ripped him apart.

As twilight descended, he'd been able to open the door. The effort to pull himself inside and shut the door had been too much for him. With no energy left, he lay on the cold pine-planked floor and stared up at the ceiling.

Oh man, he was so screwed.

His thoughts quickly turned to JJ. She was going to be so worried when he didn't show. Hell, he didn't want her to worry. She'd already had so much shit to deal with in her life. She didn't need to deal with his death too.

The pain in his head pounded harder as his thoughts turned dark. Was he going to die out here? Would they find him? Maybe days from now?

He knew they would start looking for him at first light. They would figure he'd run into trouble because he hadn't sent a message. Would they guess that time was not on their side? They knew he would have sent a message if he was delayed. Knew he didn't want to worry JJ. They must know by now he was in big trouble. Oh, JJ was going to be so pissed if he died.

Sweet JJ. His beautiful woman. He loved her so much that he couldn't remember how he'd even managed to live without her in his life.

"Hold on, Rafe. Help is coming. Don't leave me, Rafe," JJ's strong whisper curled out of the darkness, startling Rafe awake. Ribbons of pain assaulted him. Shivers racked his body.

"JJ?" he called out, hopeful that maybe she was calling him from outside the cabin. But his voice was a mere crackle. Thirst parched his throat.

No answer came. The silence descended over him like a suffocating blanket.

Shit. This was a hell of a bad way to die.

Chapter Four

"WHILE WE'RE STANDING here arguing with you, JJ, we're wasting precious time," Dan growled.

Surprise and irritation snapped through JJ as she watched Dan and Brady pile their gear into the trailers they'd hitched to their machines.

"Well, shit, guys. Had we are our own plane, we'd already be on the nearest lake to wherever the hell Rafe is working."

In the tense way they glared at her, she knew her jab had hurt.

JJ wished she'd remained quiet and just accepted that Brady and Dan wanted her to stay here to wait for help to arrive. But staying here made her feel helpless. Dan had been informed that no rescue was coming tomorrow. Resources had been pulled tight due to a perfect storm of emergencies.

A rescue chopper was searching for a group of interior campers who had gone missing in a provincial park north of Thunder Bay. There was a serious pileup due to fog on the main Trans-Canada highway and the rescue choppers were there, lifting out the injured. And a forest fire was being fought at the Manitoba-Ontario border where the rest of the rescue choppers had flown firefighters. But Dan had been assured the first available rescue chopper would be sent. Just not until probably the day after tomorrow as the pilots would all be too weary.

Dan had also called the new owner of North Country Air for help. They hadn't been able to send any search planes due to their search-and-rescue license having lapsed.

There would be no help coming from anyone.

Damn it! That same horrible helpless feeling she had experienced this past spring when Dan had gone missing was crashing in all around her. Anxiety curled through her like a horrible snake. She could feel her thoughts begin to tumble out of control. The familiar panic screamed through her head.

No! This was not the time to freak out. At least not in front of Brady and Dan. If they knew she was going into panic mode, one of them would stay here and she just knew that Rafe needed both of them out looking for him.

"Please, JJ. Stay and man the satellite phone in case Rafe calls. If he shows, let us know. When we find him, we will call you," Brady said.

His face and tone had softened, but Dan continued to look grim. JJ nodded and stepped away from the machines.

Moments later, Brady and Dan roared off on the main trail, their red taillights disappearing behind the thick white mist that was draped over the ranch and surrounding areas.

Cold, damp autumn air speared through JJ as she headed back across the yard to the house. Fear for Rafe's safety made her cry and as she entered the mudroom she heard the phone ringing.

Rafe?

Her heart hammered against her chest as she hurried down the hall and ran into the office to catch the caller. Hopefully she wasn't too late.

Rafe awoke to the sound of a scream. It rocked through him like a jolt of lightning and he opened his eyes. He was greeted to a stream of moonlight as it shone through one of the cabin's two windows. The scream came again and he relaxed as he recognized the sound.

It was an owl. It wasn't the traditional hoot, but a screech that accompanies an owl in heat.

Shit. What he wouldn't do to be back at the ranch and in the welcome embrace of JJ. Rafe swallowed against the sting of tears that suddenly blurred his vision. Emotions bubbled up from his chest and he wanted to cry. Wanted to pound his fists into something and ask what the hell had he done wrong that his life would end like this? Just yesterday...or maybe it had been the day before, he'd thought how lucky he was in having JJ, this ranch and such good partners like Dan and Brady.

Man, things sure did change in an instant. It made him realize that life was way too precious. He'd be sure to remember that...if he got out of this alive.

He trembled beneath another assault of shivers.

Fever. His leg must be infected. He should loosen the tourniquet or it might cut the blood flow. He tried to roll onto his side to make it easier to reach down to his belt, but he couldn't so much as move.

He was screwed. From somewhere far off an odd sound broke the silence. A motor?

Was he beginning to hallucinate? Most likely. He listened but could hear nothing except his heavy breathing. He tried to rein in his painful gasps and for a short few seconds there was silence.

And then something.

There. An engine? Plane maybe?

Shit! If he could just get outside, pile together some wood and get a signal fire going.

The urge to do exactly that was so strong he actually imagined himself standing there in front of a wall of fire. Heat blasted against him. His face felt so hot. Perspiration dripped into his eyes. He blinked them away.

"Hey, glad you're finally awake. What the hell you been doing with yourself?" Dan's voice crashed through the orange flames.

Rafe felt disoriented. Why could he hear Dan? What was going on? Darkness drifted over him. Everything went silent.

"The wound is infected. We need to cauterize it."

Hell, was that Brady talking? Rafe figured he must be hallucinating. Had to be.

Suddenly Brady's face hovered into view. He was smiling. It was a tight smile. Was he concerned?

"Everything is going to be all right, man. We've got a rescue plane coming. All we need to do is hoist you onto this litter and head down to the lake and into the plane, but it's going to hurt like a bitch when we move you," Brady said.

"But you can handle it, right, Rafe?" Dan was here now, too.

They'd found him!

Emotions thick and raw came out of nowhere, and hot tears blurred Rafe's vision. Oh man, he was going to lose it. He was going to start bawling like a freaking baby.

"Dan, grab him under his arms. I'll grab his legs."

Strong hands slid under his armpits. Another set slid around his ankles.

Man, he was not dreaming? This was really happening?

"At the count of three," Brady said.

"One."

Rafe braced himself.

"Two."

Hell, he was not a baby. How bad could the pain be? Certainly not any worse than what he'd already endured.

"Three."

Searing pain slashed through Rafe as he was lifted through the air. He screamed. Blackness hovered at the edges of his vision. Then nothing.

I CAN LAND THIS PLANE. I have to. For Rafe.

JJ's shoulders were so tight, she swore if someone tapped her there, her flesh would shatter into a zillion pieces. Her nerves crackled with apprehension as she gazed out the window and looked over the rugged tree line below. Gusts of wind pummelled the plane, jerking them back and forth.

Shoot! Why had she allowed Kaley to talk her into flying?

She still could not believe that when she'd picked up the phone, it had been Kaley who had overheard her new boss grumble about not having the required license in place to send out a plane do a search-and-rescue.

Upon further questions, Kaley had discovered the call had come from Moose Ranch. She had been in the air within the hour and had reached the ranch way before the crack of dawn. By then, seven hours had passed since Brady and Dan had left. During that time JJ received word from Brady that they had found Rafe, and he was injured.

Her gut had twisted in agony at the news. But she had managed to keep it together, letting Brady know that Kaley was on the way with her plane. Brady had given his coordinates and. upon inspecting the topographical map, JJ discovered a lake nearby where they could land the plane and get Rafe out fast.

Kaley had insisted JJ fly the plane due to the fact Kaley was running on no sleep for more than twenty hours. She'd said the alertness required for a search-and-rescue landing was shot, but Kaley didn't look too tired to her. Reluctantly, JJ had agreed to fly under Kaley's tutelage. But what if she did something wrong? What if she crashed the plane into the lake?

She had only landed the plane once.

"There it is. Smaller than I thought," Kaley mumbled as she checked the compass and then pointed out the window at an area down below that appeared to be a black puddle, its sides shrouded in white mist.

Good lord! How was she going to land the plane on that? She would be going in blind. It was still too dark.

"Bank to the left and go down a bit lower so we can get a look for possible obstructions in the water," Kaley instructed.

"There's practically no visual and isn't it too dark?" JJ gasped as she began to circle around and slowly descended.

"It's always a risk landing some place you are not familiar with. The sky will be lightening soon and by the time you have circled around a couple of times to check the visual you'll see enough to land."

The woman's confidence irritated JJ. She almost glared at her instructor, wanting to insinuate to Kaley that she had to be crazy. There was no way a few minutes would make a difference in light.

JJ kept her mouth shut. She could only hope Kaley knew what she was talking about.

Good grief! With her many years of flight experience, Kaley *must* know what she was talking about?

Several minutes passed as JJ followed further instructions, bringing the plane lower and lower.

"I don't see anything," Kaley muttered.

No shit.

"Okay, circle to the other end of the lake and come in right down the middle. According to topographical map the lake is deep. Doesn't show any islands either. You should have enough room for a safe landing."

No islands? She hadn't even thought about that.

"*Should* have enough room?" JJ gasped. *Oh my God*!

"Hey, sweetie. Nothing is ever one hundred percent safe. We do the best we can under whatever circumstances are given. Right?"

JJ nodded vigorously. Panic wiggled through her.

"You can do it. I have the utmost confidence in you."

Well, at least *someone* had confidence. JJ licked her dry lips and cleared her throat. She turned the plane again and headed lower. She glanced down, totally surprised that the mist appeared to be lessening and the lake had changed from a black pond to silver of about half a mile long and a quarter-mile wide.

"Should I not straighten up?" JJ asked.

The treeline grew closer. And closer. Perspiration blossomed over her forehead.

"You're doing fine, JJ. Keep dropping."

Man, this was nuts. If she got any lower, she would be able to reach out and touch the freaking treetops.

A crosswind slammed into the plane shoving them sideways. JJ swore.

Kaley chuckled. "Typical newbie." She tossed JJ a glance and smiled.

"No offense meant."

JJ refused to answer. Kaley had to be nuts — or maybe she was just suicidal dropping so low?

JJ's adrenaline pumped anxiety through her like a runaway piston. Her heart crashed against her chest a mile a minute. Surprise burst inside her as sunshine glinted off the windshield, momentarily blinding her. To the east, the sun peeked over the towering pine treetops, casting a silvery glow over the sky. Suddenly Kaley straightened in her chair, fully alert.

"Okay, it is going to be tight, so I need you to follow my instructions without question. Pretend I am the instrument panel. Trust it before you trust yourself. Do you remember that from your lessons?"

JJ nodded.

Many a pilot had crashed their plane when caught in the darkness or in fog because they had gone with their instincts thinking the plane was going up, yet it was actually going down. That she had to trust the plane's instruments had been drilled into JJ early in her lessons.

"Okay, bank ten degrees to the right," Kaley ordered.

JJ held her breath and did as she was instructed.

"Okay. Good. Now just a bit lower."

Oh boy, she hoped Kaley knew what she was doing.

The sound of an approaching plane had Brady shouting to Dan on the front end of the litter to pick up speed. It had been torturously slow-going as the two of them carried Rafe. The area around the lake, which was about a quarter of a mile from the cabin, was heavily forested, with no trails. Branches ripped into his face and up ahead of him Dan cursed.

When they had found Rafe, unconscious and bleeding on the cabin floor, they had quickly cauterized the ugly wound, and tried to get him hydrated and warm. But Brady knew from the paleness of Rafe's face and his uneven breathing that they needed to get Rafe to a hospital.

When Brady had found an area where the satellite phone worked, he'd been beyond relieved when JJ had told him her instructor from North Country Air was on her way to the ranch. He had given JJ their coordinates.

Later, he had hailed JJ again and the pilot had informed him they could land a float plane in the nearby lake at first light.

Heck, JJ *had* been right. Moose Ranch needed a plane. In Rafe's condition, they would have had a bad time securing him in a trailer and bringing him out for hours over the trails. The rough ride might have killed him.

"I see the lake. Just up ahead," Dan called out.

From the makeshift stretcher, Rafe groaned. His face was deathly white against the darkness of the forest, and Brady's stomach twisted with unease.

The roar of engines just above made him jump.

They broke out of the forest just in time to see the white plane's large pontoons slap against the water. Hell, the pilot sure did know her stuff. She came in nice and slow and ran right down the middle, hitting the water with a huge silver splash, sending several Canada geese soaring skyward. They squawked loudly with irritation at being disturbed.

Dan and Brady watched as the plane moved slowly to the other end of the lake and made a tight turn.

"They're looking for us," Dan commented.

Brady grabbed the white undershirt he had removed from himself back at the cabin knowing they might need some form of a signal for the plane and started frantically waving the shirt. Dan grabbed some softball-sized rocks and threw them into the water. The waving of white and the splashing of rocks would hopefully get their attention.

His phone rang and Brady reached for it.

"We've got you in our sights. We'll be right there." It was the pilot, Kaley.

"That was a great landing." Brady acknowledged.

"You can thank JJ. She's the one who landed the plane."

Brady was stunned. Surprise mixed with pride.

Un-freaking-believable. What the hell was JJ doing landing a plane in such dire circumstances?

"ETA. One minute. Out." The phone went quiet

Brady shoved his phone back into its holster. Anger gripped him and he could barely think straight as he watched the plane rumble closer. The lake didn't appear to have any debris that would tangle with the giant pontoons, but the wings would prevent JJ from getting too close to shore, so he tried to figure out how they were going to get Rafe on board without jostling him too much. He especially would like to keep Rafe's injured leg out of the water, but it might not be possible.

From his vantage he could now clearly see JJ. Her features were tight as she concentrated on slowing the plane. Seconds later the engines ceased and the forest fell into silence.

A moment went by and then the door opened and Kaley appeared. She waved at them and then she tossed a yellow object, the size of a large box, out of the plane. It landed on the water with a splash and a loud hissing sound followed. The item turned into a rubber raft as it quickly inflated.

Wow! The woman came prepared. An instant later, Kaley jumped into the raft, paddle in hand.

Okay, so maybe he should not be so pissed off at the instructor. It appeared she knew what she was doing. He suddenly realized that this woman, with her years of experience, and being a flight instructor, might be a damned good influence for JJ. Hell, JJ might know what she was talking about after all. Damned if he was going to admit his realization to her. At least not just yet.

Chapter Five

SHE NEEDED TO TAKE some first aid courses, JJ thought as she lay on the hospital bed beside Rafe and stared at the window. Rain pounded against the panes, making quite the noise. But Rafe remained fast asleep due to the pain medications that the doctor had ordered.

Thankfully, Rafe had not required surgery, but he had been given a blood transfusion due to losing so much blood. He'd also been given strong antibiotics to fight the infection.

Dan and Brady had explained how they had discovered Rafe. Their ATV lights had picked up the fresh tire tread marks of his machine along a side trail, and they'd found him rather quickly once they realized he'd been heading for the cabin in that area. Had they waited for daybreak to begin the search, the ensuing rain would have made a rescue longer.

JJ said another prayer of thanks. Probably the hundredth prayer since they had arrived here two days ago. She had not left Rafe's side since then except to grab something to eat, which had not been much. She just did not have an appetite since seeing Rafe's prone figure in that life raft.

How quickly bad things could happen and it kind of destroyed her confidence knowing that everyday life was going to continue no matter what happened. Nothing was a given. Change was always happening. Good and bad.

She just wasn't sure how she could deal with knowing that everything she had — her sexy cowboys, their rustic ranch and her way of life — could vanish within the blink of an eye.

A sudden touch on her hand had her head snapping up from staring at the window to discover three bouquets of flowers plus three women.

Surprise rushed through JJ. Some of the pilots from North Country Air had come to visit!

Blue, Kaley and Kelly!

JJ made a move to crawl off the bed, but the women shook their heads urging her to stay.

"Hi guys, thanks so much for dropping by. These flowers are gorgeous," she said as the women placed their bouquets on the nearby windowsill.

"Hey, this place needed to be prettied up," Kelly said with a smile.

"Yeah, especially when you have an injured, hot cowboy on your hands. Flowers are a nice distraction when he's fast asleep," Blue said with a wink.

"How is he doing?" Kelly asked softly.

"He suffered a concussion from a fall and it appears he was chopping some firewood at one of the shelters and somehow nailed the blade into his shin. They gave him some blood, but they expect a full recovery. The doctor said he'll need some physio for his leg."

"Hmm, he doesn't strike me as the type who is going to hang around here for physio," Blue commented with a frown. She gazed at Rafe and her features softened.

"Has he woken up yet?" Blue asked.

"A few times. Not for long though. The drugs make him sleepy," JJ answered.

"Where are Brady and Dan? Back at the ranch?" Kelly asked.

"Yes, they have their chores to tend to. They said they felt useless here. So I told them to go home."

The three women nodded.

"Oh and huge congratulations on that landing," Blue suddenly exclaimed with a huge smile.

"Yeah, Kaley said you dropped onto that little lake just like a pro," Kelly complimented.

"Actually, I said she was better than a pro. She is a natural. Now if she would only set up some more flying lessons, or better yet..." Kaley winked at Kelly then returned her attention to JJ.

"You may as well start flying solo. After you get enough hours flying solo, then go for the private pilot's license. I don't see you having any problems getting it and then just keep things going until you have enough hours to get your professional license and maybe fly for North Country Air."

Panic swelled through JJ and she shook her head. No way could she get paid to fly. She just wasn't reliable with her anxiety issues.

"I'm afraid my flying days are over for now. I have a sick cowboy to tend to and the ranch to help run. Maybe I will find more time next spring."

"Chickening out?" Kaley asked in a firm voice that irritated JJ.

She tried to avert Kaley's challenging gaze, but she couldn't. The dare in her flight instructor's eyes was a direct challenge.

"As I have said on several occasions during our training sessions, I can only show you the door, sweetie. It really is up to you if you want to walk through it," Kaley chastised.

JJ sighed. Kaley was right. JJ was using Rafe and the ranch as an excuse to get out of achieving her goal.

"Okay, as soon as Rafe is settled back home and he can be left alone, I will call you."

"And?" Kaley prodded.

"We will do the test."

"Promise?" Kaley asked.

"I promise." With the fingers of her right hand, JJ motioned a cross over her heart to signify a promise.

Kaley nodded her approval. Kelly and Blue beamed with excitement. They laughed and nudged each other, satisfied with JJ's answer.

Gee, why was everybody so happy, except her? She was a bundle of nerves again. To tell the truth she was kind of excited to get back into the air again too. Landing that plane onto that little lake had been traumatic, but realizing she had actually done it ...and survived.

Priceless.

An odd chorus of women's giggles vibrated through Rafe's brain. The laughs were followed by voices. Soft, happy, pleasant voices. For a few minutes he tried to slip back into the dark quiet; but laughter kept tugging him upward past the layers of sleep and into a new layer of pain.

The pain wasn't too bad. It was a hell of a lot better than when he had been in that cabin. Much better than the violent ride when he'd been carried through the forest by Dan and Brady.

Then there had been that plane ride. It had made him sick as all get-out. Although he'd been placed on the floor near the rear of the plane, he'd still been able to hear the conversation between Rafe and Brady about JJ flying the plane.

Rafe grinned. That had been one wild hallucination. JJ didn't know how to fly a plane.

Suddenly he realized the women's voices were gone. Extreme quietness followed. He didn't like the silence. It made him think he was back at the cabin.

Alone. Helpless. Dying.

His gut suddenly twisted as another thought hit him. Maybe he had dreamed his rescue? He must have because *JJ. Did. Not. Know. How. To. Fly. A. Plane.*

A burst of panic roared through him. His eyes flew open. Darkness greeted him.

Shit! It had been a dream. He needed to get to his ATV and get some help. He cursed beneath his breath, tried to turn onto his side, but a lightning blast of pain pierced his head and his injured leg hurt like hell. He stopped moving and cursed again.

Light flickered on overhead and Rafe stared up at a fluorescent lamp. Confusion wrapped around his brain. What the hell?

Something warm settled over his hand.

"Shh, everything is all right. You're safe now, Rafe." A soft, intimate voice curled around his senses like a protective blanket.

Suddenly, JJ materialized right there in front of him. He realized she lay right beside him on a bed. Her warm body heat melted into his entire left side.

"JJ?" he whispered. His voice sounded rough and raw.

"Yes, it's me. Brady and Dan found you."

Wow. He was safe. He hadn't been dreaming?

He moved his head to look around. The pain shot through his brain, but he gazed around anyway. On his right side, he noticed that he was hooked up to an IV. He figured a catheter too. A bunch of fancy flowers in plastic vases along with cards and even a big balloon that said "Get Well Soon" sat on the windowsill. There were daisies. Red roses. Carnations.

Rain pelted the windows behind the bouquets. It was dark outside. The clock on a nearby wall said seven.

"Where are we?"

"Hospital in Thunder Bay. We flew straight to the city when Kaley checked you out as I was flying the plane."

Confusion rocked him. That conversation between Dan and Brady ripped into his brain again. Not possible. He must have heard her wrong. Heard them wrong.

"She said the belt you used as a tourniquet is what saved your life. The doctor said the same thing. You knicked a main artery with the ax."

He had saved his own ass?

Weariness tugged at him. His eyelids felt heavy. Shit. He wanted to stay awake.

"Need to get out of here. Gotta get back...ranch...work," his words slurred. What had he been about to say?

"Sleep, Rafe. Sleep. Then we will get you out of here."

Her sweet voice lured him back into the deep dark world of sleep.

"TOMORROW IS THE BIG day," Dan said as he polished off a third helping of JJ's scrumptious freshly made pumpkin pie. Damn, she sure did make a great pie.

JJ gazed up from where she was doing the dishes at the kitchen sink, a huge smile on her pretty pink lips.

"I still cannot believe that Rafe let us talk him into staying in the city to continue his physiotherapy," she said.

"I think he realized he would get better faster if he followed doctor's orders," Brady replied. He had been reading a two week old newspaper, a luxury they rarely indulged in due to the fact there were no convenience stores out here.

"I hope he remembers to grab a newspaper for me before he gets the ride with North Country Air," Brady complained.

"Do you see what happens when you're exposed to the outside world? You are already back to being addicted to the news world." Dan teased.

"And addicted to takeout coffee too, Brady. I heard you on the call last night with Rafe asking him to bring you back a coffee with that newspaper. Tossing my coffee over for a takeout. Tsk. Tsk," JJ said with a fake scowl.

Dan laughed as JJ dug a clump of dish-soap bubbles and tossed it at Brady. The bubbles landed smack on top of his head.

"Good aim," Brady commented dryly. He brushed the tuft of bubbles away, his gaze suddenly turning dark and husky.

Uh. Oh. Dan recognized that look. His senses went into alert mode.

Brady wanted JJ, and he wanted her now.

"Who knew tossing around bubbles would turn you on, Brady?" Dan commented.

JJ having returned to her dishes, hadn't noticed Brady's reaction. But she did tense at Dan's comment.

The squeak of Brady's chair as he stood shot awareness through Dan. He caught Brady's intense gaze and his nod toward JJ.

An invitation to join him in having sex with JJ. Dan acknowledged it with a slight nod, his cock growing hard so quickly it hurt, but in a nice way.

"I have good aim too, JJ. Very good aim." Brady was now standing behind JJ, gyrating his hips against her bottom. She stopped washing the dishes and Dan heard a couple of sweet, soft gasps from her.

Dan's cock pressed hard against his pants. Man, he always reacted to her sensual sounds.

"Do you remember when I took you here up on the kitchen counter?" Brady murmured. JJ nodded.

Wow. They had done it in here? He wondered when. Anticipation roared through him.

Brady's hands slipped beneath her armpits and around to her front. Dan knew what Brady was doing. Unbuttoning her blouse.

"Let's let Dan have a little taste of you," Brady said. A moment later his hands were on her shoulders. Slowly, he turned JJ around to face Dan.

Her blouse hung open, revealing her bared breasts. Since being here, and with them around, she rarely wore a bra, knowing it would only be in the way when of one of them wanted to take her.

JJ's face was flushed with excitement as Brady's mouth slid against her neck. Her eyes closed as he kissed her.

Dan stepped forward and positioned himself in front of JJ. Reaching out, he slid his hands inside her blouse and cupped her breasts. She shivered and moaned. Her mounds were hot and firm, fitting perfectly in his palms. His mouth watered as his gaze lowered.

Her nipples...he licked his lips. He leaned forward, bent his head and sucked one tight warm nipple into his mouth. She hissed and her hands flew to Dan's pants zipper. Her fingers were quick, and the rasp of his zipper lowering followed.

He groaned as her hand wrapped snugly around his rigid erection. Oh man, every time she held his shaft it was as if he had died and gone to heaven. Yeah, he could live like this, forever.

JJ struggled to keep standing as Brady pressed his thick erection against her bottom. Despite the fact that both men were wearing jeans, their body heat burned through her clothing and ignited a firestorm of need. Dan's wicked mouth sucked on her nipple and then the other. The feel of his sharp teeth as he nipped her tender nipple and his possessive grip on her breasts warned her she was in for an intense night of lovemaking. The fierce pulsing of Dan's penis in her hand had her moaning softly into Brady's mouth.

Brady's kisses along the length of her neck alternated between soft and rough as if he were trying to make up his mind about something.

"I've been thinking about something," Brady murmured against her flesh.

Aha. Just as she had suspected.

"What's that?" she whispered as she held tight to Dan's cock, while he settled at her breast.

"You need to be punished for not telling us about your wanting to learn how to fly."

Surprise washed over her.

"Oh?" she breathed.

Dan's mouth tensed around her nipple. Brady had captured his interest.

"You've been holding out on us, all summer. You shouldn't have done that, baby," Brady's voice had turned hoarse.

"Gotta agree with you there, Brady. A nice punishment would make me feel a whole lot better," Dan said. His voice had turned tight.

"What if I don't agree to being punished?" JJ stammered. Surely the two of them were kidding?

"Something severe. Something she won't soon forget," Brady whispered into her ear.

Mercy, why did he make a punishment sound so sensual?

Brady taunted her, his fingers moving sensuously over her belly to her pants zipper. Dan continued to suck on her nipples. She jerked beneath the pleasure and kept stroking Dan's hot shaft.

Heat seared through her as Brady unzipped her jeans, then slid them, along with her panties, lower over her hips and down her legs. Quickly, she kicked off her slippers, stepped out of her pants and panties and kicked them aside.

"It makes you hot, doesn't it? Knowing two men are going to punish you. I know it really turns me on," Brady said.

She creamed when she heard the rest of Brady's zipper lowering. Heard the rip of plastic. Caught him reaching for the vegetable oil in the cupboard and settling it on the counter. She also noticed he had placed an unused condom there as well. She tensed as he withdrew a wooden spoon from the cup that held some utensils.

"You wouldn't..." she gasped.

She yelped as he slapped her ass. A burst of pain blushed across her cheeks.

He did!

Her lower belly tightened as heat spun across her flesh. Brady smacked her ass again. Harder this time. She bucked and tried to get away but Dan's hands held tight on her hips. His mouth continued to nibble on her peaks.

Damn them! How quickly this had turned from a leisurely evening to something so...erotic.

She cried out as Brady continued to slap her ass with that wooden spoon. Heat and pain mingled. Pleasure burned across her buttocks and seared her nipples and breasts.

Suddenly Dan's face lifted. She caught his sensual gaze as he watched her yelp and buck while Brady continued to paddle her.

"You like getting spanked, I can tell," Dan whispered as his eyes grew darker and heavy-lidded with lust.

She closed her eyes as Dan moved against her. His hands slipped into her hair, his fingers tangling with the strands until erotic pain seared through her scalp. She moaned against the pain and cried out as his hips surged and his thick, long shaft drove into her wet vagina. Her muscles clenched him tight and he growled. It was an animalist sound that made her heady.

Brady cursed softly and stopped paddling her. His breathing grew heavier and she sensed he was sheathing himself. Then she heard slurping sounds as he generously laved his shaft with the oil.

Dan withdrew and his mouth melted over hers, chasing away any thoughts. JJ slid her hands around Dan's neck and drew herself deeper into his kiss.

Brady parted her cheeks, and she gasped as he pressed his cockhead against her tight sphincter. Brady's hands slipped along her waist and he held her tight.

Her anticipation soared.

She pushed her tongue into Dan's mouth. His fingers twisted tighter into her hair as he kissed her back.

She gasped as Brady's penis stretched into her ass. His shaft was hard and hot as he lodged deeper and deeper. Brady withdrew and then Dan thrust into her.

Quickly, they picked up an intoxicating rhythm. Dan pistoned into her pussy and Brady pushed his swollen flesh deeper and deeper until the wicked pinch of pleasure and pain mingled together and threatened to make her wild.

JJ struggled to hold onto her self-control for as long as she could. Maybe it was an act of defiance against her punishment. Or maybe she was being selfish, knowing the longer she held back, the more intense her orgasm would be.

But their fierce pace pushed her closer and closer to the fragile edge of bliss. She wriggled her body between theirs and gyrated her hips and enjoyed hearing them growl and groan.

But when they both thrust into her at the same time, JJ lost her thin grip on control and shattered into a bundle of agonizing pleasure. Their moans ripped through the air as she bucked harder between them.

She flew deeper and deeper into the pleasure. She loved the fiery shudders convulsing through her flesh and muscles. The perspiration sheening her skin did nothing to cool her.

They kept pistoning. Solid. Fierce. Deep, soul-wrenching strokes.

The pleasure kept coming. She was drowned in the roaring waves that spread through her like a storm.

It was sheer ecstasy.

JJ whimpered and keened and dug her nails deep into Dan's shoulders as another orgasm quickly rocked her. The pleasure burned her alive.

Cocks kept plunging and thrusting, making her twist like a mindless puppet.

Brady's hands were moving up and down her sides, his caresses soft and intimate. JJ knew he meant to calm her, but it merely intoxicated her more. Everywhere they touched her, she burned. Their body heat melted her flesh and destroyed her mind. She was one with them.

One soul. One body. Blind pleasure.

She was theirs. Completely.

It felt good to be back at the ranch, Rafe thought for the thousandth time since returning here two weeks ago. Today he was fixing the tractor that was needed to bring in the hay. Brady said it had been acting up all day yesterday, stalling now and again out in Section Thirteen, one of their largest hay-producing fields.

His leg had healed pretty well, and it had already been a month since that freak accident had waylaid him. He limped, his shin throbbed with every step, but he was on the mend, eager for the cattle drive to begin in a few days.

With October finally here, the weather had turned cold and windy with plenty of cloudy days and chilly drizzle. With the weather finally clearing over the last three days, Dan and Brady were doing the last of the haying.

Guilt assailed Rafe that they had picked up his duties, but that left him with plenty of JJ time.

Every time he looked at her, there was a curious fluttering feeling in his chest. Since that desolate day and night in that lonesome cabin when he had come face to face with the reality he might never see her again, he looked at everything differently. In the daylight, he appreciated everything. The scent of pine. The cry of the loon. The gentle lapping of water against the shoreline.

He enjoyed the bad coffee Dan made. He chuckled whenever Brady got pissed off about the eggs or the price of food. Best of all, he enjoyed helping JJ out around the kitchen. Setting the table, putting away the dishes or running out to the garden to grab her a cabbage or some turnips. It was as if he were on a high since being back.

Unfortunately, the high disappeared when he fell asleep. Almost every night, he dreamed of those two gray wolves he had seen at that cabin. He should have realized those wolves had been a message of foreboding.

Rafe also dreamed of slicing his leg open with the ax, of being helpless and in pain. He always awoke in a sweat, his heart racing a mile a minute. A sense of loss, along with a weird emotion of impending doom, followed him out of those nightmares. The only nights he didn't have bad dreams were the ones he spent with JJ. Having her lying beside him in bed seemed the healing salve he needed. He wished he could sleep with her every night. But he also knew one day he would have to face whatever fears were nibbling away at him since that accident. He sure as hell was not looking forward to it.

Chapter Six

FROM THE KITCHEN JJ had a good view of the yard. Chickadees and blue jays fluttered around the bird feeders just outside the window. In the distance, she saw the giant two-story barn with knotty pine siding, the cedar-railed corrals for some of the cows, and the adjoining sawmill.

In front of the barn's wide double doors, Rafe worked on the old blue tractor.

Bright mid-afternoon sunshine beat down on his broad bare shoulders and a sheen of sweat glistened on his back. Tanned, golden muscles flexed and rippled as he worked. His jeans hung low on his hips giving her a peek at the crack in his ass. He had the sexiest butt of all three guys. Plump and curvy. JJ liked running her hands over his smooth flesh. Loved the way his butt muscles flexed beneath her palms whenever she massaged him there.

She also realized his hair was getting long and shaggy. It gave him a dangerous look. She found his disheveled appearance to be sexy. Best of all, he was wearing his cowboy hat.

Ever since coming here to the ranch and seeing Brady's black cowboy hat that first night when she'd been drunk, she realized cowboy hats turned her on. Big time.

The dark five o'clock shadow was already hugging Rafe's cheeks and chin and her breath caught as her pussy quivered, thinking about how those rough whiskers would rasp against her pussy.

Suddenly, she craved to touch Rafe. To run her fingers over his rigid flesh and to bring his shaft deep inside her. It was a new hunger for him, she didn't understand. But ever since he had been injured, she wanted

to be near him. To be with him. To know he was still alive and that he
wanted her.

A quick glance at the kitchen clock told her it was almost
lunchtime. If she hurried, the two of them could eat outdoors, right
under the sun, and maybe afterward...

IT TOOK JJ LESS THAN fifteen minutes to whip up a lunch of roast
beef sandwiches with an accompanying fruit salad. As she let herself
out the back door and descended the steps with the picnic basket, she
sensed Rafe was already aware of her. Although she was more than
fifty yards away, she noticed his shoulders were tense as he knocked on
something inside the front area of the tractor. She liked the way the
sunlight gleamed off the sweat glistening on his back. Loved how he
suddenly looked up and watched her with predatory awareness as she
approached. Her belly fluttered as his chest muscles flexed. Her breasts
swelled against her knit top as his hungry gaze lingered on her chest.

Mercy, it appeared he might be as aroused as she was at the
prospect of something naughty happening between the two of them.

JJ swallowed as he pushed his cowboy hat higher off his forehead,
giving her a close-up view of his dark eyelashes and his heated eyes. As
she dropped the basket onto the tractor seat, he placed a tool he'd been
using onto the ground, grabbed a rag and wiped his sweaty face and
then his greasy hands.

"Hey, baby. Lunch already?"

JJ nodded, hoping he would simply take her into his arms and start
madly kissing her. He didn't. Disappointment shifted through her.

"You're just in time," Rafe said with a lopsided grin.

"For?"

"To take this baby for a ride. See if she works. I think I have fixed the problem. We can take the food with us. There's enough for both of us, isn't there?"

"Yes, plenty. Where will we go?" JJ asked.

"We'll go wherever the tractor takes us," Rafe said with a wink.

He scooped up the basket and hung it on a hook that dangled from the back of the large seat. Then he climbed up and sat down. He held out his hand to her. She placed her hand into his and he hoisted her up as if she were a feather.

He indicated she should sit in front of him, where he had left room for her on the seat. She sat down and her breath caught as he pressed against her, giving her an erotic touch of a very impressive erection against her backside. His arms came around her sides holding her hostage as he twisted the key in the ignition.

The tractor roared to life, giving off the scent of fuel fumes. Rafe grabbed the steering wheel and shifted his body even nearer. His head drew closer as well and his warm breath caressed her cheek.

"You thought I didn't notice, didn't you?" Rafe murmured into her ear. She barely heard him above the rattling purr of the engine.

JJ shivered in excitement.

"Notice what?"

"That you want a little fun under the sun. Baby, I know that sexy look you get in your eyes when you need some tender loving."

"I didn't make you a picnic lunch because I want sex from you, Rafe."

The little bugger knew her too well.

He laughed and shoved the tractor into gear. The machine lurched forward.

"Whether you want it or not, I am giving it to you," he said in a guttural voice that sent shock waves of eagerness through her.

As he drove the tractor along the well-travelled trail that meandered through the nearby forests, JJ caught glimpses of squirrels and rabbits as they scampered out of their way.

As he drove, Rafe kissed her neck. The raspy touch of his facial whiskers sparked against her flesh, a direct contrast to his plump, moist mouth.

"You steer," he whispered. He barely gave her the time to grab the wheel before his hands landed on her top button.

Oh, my. Rafe's fingers moved swiftly, until all the buttons were undone and her knit top fluttered opened. JJ trembled and held tight to the wheel as his hands cupped her bare breasts and his callused palms rubbed her sensitive nipples.

She loved the way he touched her. Tender, yet firm. Sexual heat pulsed through her as he pulled her nipples. She arched against him and moaned softly as he kissed her along the side of her neck.

"Um, Rafe," she suddenly called out as she spied a large, dark-brown silhouette standing in the middle of the trail just up ahead.

"Yeah, baby. You like?"

She yelped as he pinched her nipples and pain sparked. Then he soothed the burn with the pads of his palms. His lips nibbled on her neck sending sweet tingles down her spine.

"Oh, very nice," JJ whispered and suddenly remembered why she was trying to get Rafe's attention.

The dark silhouette loomed larger.

"How do I brake this thing?" she cried out, frantic at how fast the tractor was heading toward the giant animal that stood almost six feet high.

"Rafe?"

"Huh?" his voice was thick with arousal.

"Moose. Up ahead," she gasped.

That got his attention. Rafe cursed. She jolted as he suddenly applied the brakes and they came to an abrupt halt.

"Oh man, this is not good," he muttered as he stared at the creature.

"Why? It's just a moose. Beep the horn and he will move."

"You need to keep your voice down. He is a she. Look over that way." Rafe nodded to the left toward a swamp. Her heart melted when she saw two more moose standing belly deep in the tall reeds and cattails. Those animals were smaller in size than the one standing in the middle of the trail.

"It's mating season. There's probably a bull moose or two around here somewhere. Those smaller ones in the marsh are her offspring. Born this spring by the look of them. She'll be kicking them out as soon as she gets pregnant again. When moose are scared they might charge a human, so we'd best give her her space."

"I thought it was bears that were dangerous," JJ said as a sliver of fear rippled up her spine.

"Moose can be too. They aren't territorial, but they can attack humans if provoked, annoyed or scared. Their hooves are pointy and they can do a lot of damage if they start kicking. They have pretty flexible legs and can kick in all kinds of directions with both front and back legs. So yeah, best not to spook her more than we already have."

Rafe jammed the tractor into reverse.

"She is watching us like a hawk," JJ said, wishing she were sitting behind Rafe, instead of in front of him.

The moose looked like an oversized deer. She had a big head with a long snout and very long skinny legs. The rest of her was huge and covered in dark brown hair.

"How much do you think she weighs?"

"Six hundred, maybe seven hundred pounds. The males are even bigger and get up to a thousand pounds."

"Wow, that's a lot of moose meat."

"We try not to kill too many moose. Their population is in decline due to overhunting. But I can tell you, they do taste good in lasagna."

JJ laughed. "You and your stomach."

"Me and my stomach say we need to keep backing up. Keep an eye on her. Let me know if her ears go down or if her hackles go up."

"Hackles?" *What*?

"The hairs on the back of her neck and shoulders will puff up if she's thinking of charging us. If her hackles go up and she starts to move toward us, we're in trouble. Shit! I should have remembered to bring the rifle."

Rafe's alarm made JJ stiffen.

Wow, she hadn't realized how dangerous it could get for her guys out here. She realized they had kept her pretty isolated from the hazards of wilderness ranching, just so she wouldn't be overly concerned about them when they went out every day. Just like she'd been keeping her flying from them so they wouldn't worry about her.

JJ kept her gaze on the mother moose. She watched them and stood as stiff as a statue. But her ears thankfully didn't go down and her hackles didn't go up.

The tractor moved slowly in reverse and JJ squirmed in her seat wishing Rafe would move this contraption faster, but she understood that he was moving slowly so as not to frighten the moose into charging.

"I'm not the best at driving backward. You'd best keep your head down," he said as he clipped a few pine branches at the edge of the trail. She moved aside just in time and the branches missed her right shoulder.

Thankfully, there was another curve in the trail that blocked their view of the moose. She felt Rafe relax against her.

"That was close," he grumbled. To her surprise, there was a tremble in his voice.

"You really were scared?" she asked as he began to turn around the tractor.

"Hell, yeah. It's healthy to be scared of things that might kill you. Survival instincts."

JJ looked down and watched as his big hands twisted the wheel. A moment later he had turned the tractor around and they quickly moved along the trail back toward the ranch house.

Amazing. A strong, tough guy like Rafe had fears too. It got her thinking about her own fears. She had plenty of them. Terror of closed spaces. Panic attacks. Distress at crashing a plane?

JJ worried her bottom lip as she suddenly realized something. Had she not been working on overcoming her anxiety over the last several months and had she not had the courage to start flying lessons with Kaley, what would have happened to Rafe? Kaley might never have called that night to offer her help and JJ would not have been able to fly the plane to rescue him.

Maybe she was supposed to keep pursuing her goals? Maybe she should keep practicing her exposure therapy and continue with her flying lessons, despite her fears and anxieties?

Baby steps. Kaley's words echoed through her mind.

JJ smiled and nodded. It was time to stop hiding behind the excuse of tending to Rafe. It was time to get back to breaking through the walls of anxiety that had been wrapped around her for so many years. She had read that plenty of people conquered or dealt with their anxiety and panic issues, living with their problem on a daily basis. If those people could do it, then she surely could do it too.

"What's got you nodding like that, sweetheart?" Rafe whispered as he softly rubbed the side of his face against the side of hers. Such a tender gesture.

"I was just thinking about something," JJ said.

"What's that?" Rafe asked.

"That I want you to make love to me, right now. Right here on the trail. Right up against his tractor. Right..." Before she could finish saying right now, he brought the tractor to a complete halt, turned off the engine and tapped her shoulder.

JJ twisted around to see what he wanted and gasped as he lowered his head. Rafe caught her mouth with his warm lips and kissed her so deeply she couldn't even think straight. She reached back and clasped her hands over his knees, holding tight for balance as his tongue pushed into her mouth and stroked over her teeth. His hands slipped beneath her armpits and slid into her open top and smoothed over her breasts. His fingers tweaked her nipples until they were painfully hard peaks. His erection, a large, hard promise of things to come, pushed boldly against her ass cheeks.

JJ felt so alive. So free out here with the blue sky overhead and the moaning trees twisting in the wind. The breeze was cool and refreshing against her heated skin.

"Let's get down," Rafe whispered as he broke the kiss.

"Is it safe?" She almost didn't care if it was dangerous.

"Yeah, we're far enough away from the moose. Besides, she won't come and watch us. She's looking for action of her own."

"Like I am," she whispered.

Rafe chuckled as he hopped down, and then helped her off the tractor. The instant JJ's feet hit the ground, Rafe speared his fingers through her hair and held her head.

His eyes were dark and intense as he studied her.

"Did I ever tell you that I really, really love you, JJ?" he said in a soft, tender voice that curled her toes.

JJ blinked with surprise.

Sure, he muttered that he loved her while they had sex, but this time was different. He was different. Very forceful. Sincere.

"I love you too, Rafe. With all my heart."

He smiled and the smile brightened his eyes. He lowered his head and he stroked his tongue over her lips until her mouth was tingling. Then leisurely, ever so torturously slow, he dipped his head and kissed a line of fire along the left side of her neck and then sparked more kisses across her collarbone.

JJ gasped as he pushed her against the tire of the tractor, her ass pressing against the hard bumpy rubber. She shuddered as his mouth found her right nipple and he sucked it between his lips. Pleasure zipped through her as his raspy five o'clock shadow burned her flesh.

Sensations pummelled her as his other hand squeezed and massaged her other breast. His fingers tweaked and gently rubbed her nipple until she was moaning into his mouth.

Then he moved his hand and mouth away, leaving both nipples throbbing and aching. He stepped away from her and she lowered her pants and panties and kicked them off and then watched as he undid his pants and dropped his underwear.

JJ trembled at the sight of his large shaft as it stuck straight out at her. An erotic weave of veins pulsed along his thick flesh. He reached into his shirt pocket and withdrew a packaged condom. The rip of foil followed and a moment later he was sheathed.

Her heart beat a mile a minute as he gazed at her with pure lust and love shining in his eyes.

"Come here, baby," Rafe breathed.

She took a step closer to him, and his raw scent filled her nostrils making her heart pick up speed. His hand moved down to between her thighs. She moaned as he dipped two of his fingers into her wet vagina. He removed his fingers and then rubbed her cream over his condom. He did that several times until the top quarter of his condom was generously lubed with her cream.

Then he reached out and took her hands into his. Rafe's eyes were glazed with lust as he held her fingers tight and pushed her back against the tractor tire again.

"When I had that accident, you are what kept me going," he whispered.

Me?

"I heard your voice. Heard you telling me to hold on. That help was coming. And for me not to leave you."

"I kept thinking all of that. I was so worried. I just wanted you home with me."

Was it possible they had some sort of magical bond? Or had it just been in his hallucinated state that he'd thought he'd heard her?

"Good to know you were thinking it," Rafe murmured.

JJ gasped and all her thoughts disintegrated as Rafe's warm mouth melted over hers and his stiff cockhead touched her sensitive clitoris. Pleasure shimmered in bundles as his velvet tongue dashed past her lips and she met him with sensual movements of her own.

He groaned, liking what she did to him with her tongue. The guttural sound of his voice fired her blood and she kissed him harder, quickly drowning into the fiery vibrations.

Instinctively, she gyrated her hips, diving into the pleasure he created. He matched her movements while continuing to massage her tender clit.

Tension built quickly deep inside JJ. When Rafe let go of her hands, she slid them around his waist and caressed his ass. His cheeks were full and taut and she loved the way his muscles flexed beneath her fingers.

Rafe rubbed her clit harder and faster whipping up a frenzy of pleasure. Suddenly she could hold back no longer as her body and mind exploded into a mirage of mindless shudders.

JJ cried into Rafe's mouth and shook at the impact.

Quickly, he thrust into her. His solid cock pierced deep into her vagina and she welcomed his thickness. She loved the tight way her muscles clenched around his perfect intrusion. He withdrew and pistoned into her again.

She met his every plunge, bucking her hips against his. His flesh was firm and long as it slid in and out of her like a steel piston. Every push went deeper and harder. Every plunge sent more spirals of pleasure through her.

She shuddered against him as he came apart with her. He drove into her like a man possessed. A man who claimed. A man who loved.

Stars sparkled behind her eyes as she kept bucking against him. They kept up the mindless pace until they were both spent, their breaths crashing through the autumn air.

As their climaxes ebbed, Rafe stayed inside of her, his cock throbbing and hot as he wrapped his arms around her. He held her tenderly, his soft lips gently kissing hers as he muttered her name over and over again.

Slowly, every so slowly, JJ's thoughts began to re-form and her body hummed with satisfaction. She remembered what he had said moments earlier, that she had kept him going during his accident. She truly was important to him. That thought filled her heart with warmth and love. She already knew she could never leave them or this ranch, but him telling her what he'd experienced only solidified her decision to remain here forever with her three men.

Chapter Seven

BY THE TIME THE CATTLE drive rolled around, Rafe was good to go. JJ noticed he barely limped now and the pain lines etching his mouth were gone. Relief for Rafe made her happy, and when she was happy, she baked.

The guys were leaving this morning and last night she had made them a cornbread cake, a bunch of homemade granola bars and apple fritters, and then this morning she'd whipped up two loaves of zucchini cake using zucchini from the garden. The cakes were ready to take out of the oven and they would have no shortage of sweets during their week long cattle drive.

She eyed the six bear-proof steel storage containers that held the non-perishable food supplies she had already packed.

Mentally, she checked off her list.

For breakfast, she had packed for each of them pancake mix, maple syrup, dried blueberries, freeze dried strawberries. Plenty of instant coffee. Whitener. Sugar. Corn meal and wheatlets. Powdered cheese for the cornmeal and canned peaches and pears to complement the wheatlets.

For lunch they had plenty of canned soups, cowboy beans, and canned vegetables, rice and potatoes. Supper they had their choice of canned and freeze-dried stew, pasta and preserved tomato sauce.

JJ smiled as she grabbed her oven mitts. And, of course, they had their sweets.

Since they would be working on their own most of the time, each of them also had their own ultra-large coolers, which contained fresh fruits and vegetables, steaks and other perishable items.

It would take six to seven days get all the cattle to the railroad area where arrangements had been made for the train to stop and have the cattle loaded on the cars. Then it would take an estimated one-day ride on their machines to get back to her.

JJ's breath backed up as she thought about their reunion, but there cows and their newborns that needed tending. She had also made arrangements for daily flight instructions with Kaley. JJ had wanted to bring up the subject to the guys many times over the past couple of weeks, but she just didn't have the nerve.

Besides, they would just worry about her if they knew she had resumed her lessons. They needed their full attention on the cattle drive, not on her flying a plane.

JJ opened the oven and retrieved one of the loaves. She had just set it upon the top of the stove when she heard the stomping of feet up the back stairs.

Oh shoot. They were already coming inside to get their gear. She had hoped to hide the cakes until they were cool and then wrap them. She removed the other cake and set it beside the other one. Maybe if she hurried she could hide them...

"Hey baby. The machines are ready to go. Do we have everything packed? Oh it smells good in here. Let's eat," Dan said as he entered the kitchen and his gaze snapped onto the two loaves.

JJ laughed. Unbelievable!

"You guys just ate an hour ago."

"Are those for me?" Dan said with a wink.

"Not so fast, Buster. They are mine," Rafe growled as he entered the kitchen right behind Dan.

"Sorry guys, but those cakes are all for me. Where's the knife? Gonna have me a piece and some coffee. You know how I love steaming hot cake," Brady added as the three men crowded in around JJ and the cakes.

As Brady went to open the knife drawer, JJ grabbed a wooden spoon and gently smacked Brady on his knuckles.

"Ouch!" He gasped in mock hurt and held his hand to his chest.

Rafe and Dan laughed.

"I will make the coffee. You guys go sit down in the living room and go over your plans one more time before you head out," JJ instructed as she shooed them out of her kitchen waving her spoon at them.

They laughed and settled themselves in the living room. She figured getting them distracted with work might allow her to save at least one of those cakes and allow it to cool a bit before she cut it up and wrapped the pieces.

"Coffee coming right up," she called out. She should have known they would want some cake before heading out. She just never learned.

Within fifteen minutes, JJ had a plate piled high with steaming cake slices and the guys were supplied with coffee. She settled between Dan and Rafe who sat on the living room sofa. They spread a map across her lap and showed her the areas each of them would be working. She'd already been shown all this information but the men were so proud of their spread that their excitement was always contagious, and she never tired of gazing at the maps.

"I left a list of the barn chores that need to be done out on the workshop bench in the barn," Brady said from where he sat on the lounge chair across from them.

JJ nodded. "Good."

Over the summer, they had been showing her the routine she would follow when they were gone. She doubted she needed to look at the list. JJ knew what to do. Feeding the cattle in the pens. Cleaning out their stalls. Putting down fresh straw. Making sure the temperature didn't get too cold in the barn. She knew how to run the generators in case the electricity went out. She had also been busy canning some of the vegetables from the garden and storing them in the cellar for the winter. She would do more while they were gone.

Before the guys returned, she hoped to learn how to make pumpkin pie from one of those huge orange pumpkins out in the garden. She also had a little surprise in store for them when they got back. She bit her lower lip as an excited tremble whispered through her. She could hardly wait for them to come home, and they hadn't even left yet.

"Lady, I know that look," Brady said in a thick voice.

JJ's breath caught at his hot gaze. Dan and Rafe stopped talking as they focused their attention on her.

"All I am thinking about will happen when you get back. No time now. It will be that much sweeter with the three of you when you return."

They groaned in disappointment. She could not believe she was saying no to sex. She should have her head examined. But she had everything timed perfectly for today. She needed to keep her men on their schedule, so she could stick to hers.

"Come on, eat up. The cake is getting cold and the daylight is burning."

She grabbed a slice of cake and took a big bite, following it up with a sip of sweet coffee. She did have to admit she was a good baker. The guys followed her lead and began to eat. She was thankful, at least for now, that her baking took precedence over sex.

Yeah, she really should have her head examined.

THE DAY DRAGGED WITHOUT having to make lunch and supper for the guys. Kaley would be arriving late afternoon and JJ utilized the time doing the required chores in the barn and tending to the cattle. She had to admit that she did feel sorry for the cows, knowing that they would be spending the upcoming winter months outdoors in the cold elements, getting fattened up on the hay and nutritional supplements the guys would bring out to them on a daily basis. But when the warm weather arrived and the snow melted, the cows would have tons of grass to eat. The guys had told her that when the cows were five years old they would be ready for market.

Many of the young cows that had been calved earlier this year were already in the various meadows surrounding the ranch, weaned from their mothers. Well, at least the cows on Moose Ranch had it better than the commercial variety, who were fed corn and other supplements, growth hormones, antibiotics and slaughtered within two years of their life.

But JJ tamped down on her sorrow. This organic beef ranch was a way of life. Her way of life. She could not imagine being anywhere else but here.

AS SHE EMERGED FROM the semidarkness of the barn, she shielded her eyes from the mid-October afternoon sunshine. The low drone of an approaching plane made her pick up her speed.

Kaley was here!

JJ rushed into the ranch house, washed her hands in the bathroom, grabbed a clean top and warm track pants out of the laundry basket where she had folded her clothing earlier, quickly changed, grabbed her gear and headed back out.

She made it down to the dock just in time to help Kaley secure the float plane to the dock. Kaley watched patiently as JJ did the external preflight inspection and complemented her on a job well done when she was finished.

"I was serious back at the hospital. You really are a natural at this. And you should start flying solo too. One more time with me today, and then you're on your own. Okay?"

JJ nodded. Kaley's praise made JJ's cheeks heat with a blush.

"Go on in. I'll cast off," Kaley instructed.

Nervousness snapped through JJ as she stepped on board the plane and lost the wide-open space to the steel wall interior.

Thankfully, she didn't experience the overwhelming, killing anxiety that had haunted her during the earlier flight lessons, but it was uncomfortable anxiety just the same. She needed to keep her nervousness under control before it screwed with today's plans. Tossing her knapsack onto a back seat, JJ moved up the aisle into the cockpit and settled into the pilot's chair. The familiar smell of fuel and oil soothed her rattled nerves.

When Kaley joined her, JJ began the interior pre-flight inspection, glad for the now familiar routine that would help her overcome her anxiety. Moments later, JJ's heart leapt with excitement as she rushed the bush plane over the choppy waves. When the pontoons left the water, the feeling of lightness made JJ smile.

Wow! She was flying again. Who would have thought?

After they reached altitude, JJ took the opportunity to gaze down at the lush beauty surrounding them. The canopy of trees was abound with colors of fall foliage. Vibrant green from pine, spruce and other evergreens. Crimson-red maple trees. Bright-yellow birch. Rusty orange, browns and golden hues from other trees.

The abundance of lakes were like blue buttons in the colorful fabric of autumn.

"Breathtaking, isn't it?" Kaley said as she peered out her window.

"I never knew such beauty existed," JJ admitted.

"Most people don't. Consider yourself one of the world's bravest souls, JJ. Never underestimate what you can do, despite any lingering doubts." JJ caught the wistful tone in Kaley's voice as she said that last sentence.

"You are speaking from experience, aren't you?" JJ prodded.

With the exception of that the one time Kaley had opened up about the car crash that had caused all her scars, she'd been a secretive and mysterious woman.

To JJ's disappointment, Kaley merely nodded.

"Just remember. Baby steps. Always baby steps. Sometimes you wobble and fall, or take a few steps backward. But then you get right back up and do more baby steps. With that mantra, you can conquer anything."

An unfamiliar confidence soared inside JJ as she focused her attention back to flying the plane. She liked this new feeling of accomplishment. She liked it a lot.

AS BRADY TOSSED HUNKS of canned ham into the pot of vegetable soup, he watched the flickering flames of his campfire and waited for Rafe and Dan to join him. The past few days had melted together with the hard manual labor of rounding up the cattle.

Instead of using horses, they used the sturdy four-wheelers to guide the animals along the corralled paths that led from the meadows toward the large holding area by the railroad line. They had been doing this same cattle drive route for several years now and it never ceased to amaze Brady at how much thought and work had gone into designing their network of fenced meadows with adjoining pathways and carving out quite a profitable living in the middle of the vast Northern Ontario wilderness where few people lived.

He was proud of the herds he'd brought to the holding pens. The black beef were sturdy, lean and healthy. Until last year, they'd grown just black Angus. But then they'd decided on trying out the brown breed too. It appeared they were well-suited to the rugged wilderness environment. In another four years there would be a mix of black and brown Angus. Both varieties would bring a good price at the market. City folks were looking for prime organic beef and they paid a pretty penny for the fantastic taste and all the hard work that went into creating free range, antibiotic-free steaks for their table.

A flurry of activity from beside him had Brady reaching for his rifle. Two chipmunks rushed out of the nearby foliage, one hot on the heels of the other one. Brady relaxed and leaned the rifle back against the fallen log where he sat. It wasn't the greatest idea to be exposed to the elements out here like this.

The dark silhouette of an old cabin stood nearby, but the roof had caved in during last year's heavy snow. A replacement shelter was on next year's agenda. They planned on getting a solid cabin that would hold under the extreme weather.

Until then, they'd set up camp in the small meadow by the dilapidated cabin and were using a large canvas tent to sleep and cooked their meals out in the open.

With darkness descending, the cattle began to fall silent with only an occasional moo. Somewhere far off a loon cried a lonely song and overhead the dark blue rolling clouds blew in an icy wind. He would not be surprised if they got some snow overnight.

An unexpected snowstorm had caught them off guard during their second year here. The storm had dumped a good foot, trapping them. Thankfully at daybreak the warm sunshine had melted the snow or they would have had to abandon their vehicles and caught a ride with their cattle in one of the many railway cars headed into Thunder Bay. Then they would have flown back with North Country Air.

To avoid any surprise snow, they'd made the cattle drive a week earlier every since then. So far, they'd been lucky and hadn't experienced another storm like that one.

Over the past weeks, he'd been thinking a lot about JJ and her desire to fly. She hadn't mentioned it anymore, so he had kept quiet. Except of course when he looked at the transportation bills. He couldn't help but be vocal at the new prices.

JJ's idea of getting a plane for ranch use was a good one. But it just didn't sit right with him taking advantage of her. Having her up in the air at the mercy of the elements and whatever else that could go wrong with a plane made him kind of crazy with worry.

She sure had changed from that vulnerable, frightened woman who had shown up here almost a year ago. Now, she was comfortable around them. She demanded sex, which she appeared to enjoy immensely. He'd also noticed that her anxiety and panic attacks were almost nonexistent now. Unless she was able to hide her attacks better from them.

Brady nibbled on his bottom lip and stirred the soup. It smelled good. His stomach growled and his mouth watered with anticipation. He hoped the guys would get here soon because if they didn't, there wouldn't be any soup left for them.

Well, at least he wouldn't be stuck washing the dishes tonight. Cattle drive rule. First one into camp did the cooking. The second one in got the night off. The last guy in washed the dishes.

Happiness whispered through Rafe as he spied the campfire flickering up ahead. He had just finished driving his last herd into one of the holding pens and his stomach was pretty damned empty. He had left his vehicle parked out by the pens opting to do a bit of walking to give his leg some exercise. It still went stiff by the end of the day, and all that sitting while he angled cattle out of the meadows and along the trails to get them here made his leg that much harder to keep limber.

It didn't help any when some of the cattle were stubborn, refusing to be herded along the fenced trails that would lead them to the railway yard. Perhaps, instinctively they knew they would be heading to the slaughterhouse. Or maybe they just enjoyed the freedom of grass lush meadows opposed to the narrow fenced trails.

Those stubborn types of cattle reminded him of himself and Brady and Dan and the reason they had left the rat race of city life. They had come here to pursue freedom. To live off the land and to be their own bosses.

He exhaled a white plume of mist and quickened his pace. Damn cold night. But just one more night out here. Early tomorrow morning the train was scheduled the stop here, and they could begin loading the cows.

It would be an all-day event. By nightfall they would drive the machines along the trails that led to another cabin about ten miles from here. As his luck would have it, that cabin would be the same shelter where he had had his freak accident. He sure was not looking forward to reliving his nightmares at that place.

He spied Brady sitting by the fire, eagerly sipping from a steaming mug. Brady nodded toward a lidded pot set on a steel grill amidst the campfire.

"Vegetable soup with slabs of ham. There is some sliced bread and I've spread butter on them." Brady nodded to a nearby tree stump they were using as a table.

"Damn, that smells good. Is Dan back?" He asked as he scooped the soup into a tin cup and eagerly grabbed a thick slice of buttered bread.

"Looks like you got the night off, my man."

Rafe grunted his thanks. It would be a relief to just sit, stare at the fire and think of JJ and eat.

"Finished my herd. You?" Rafe asked.

Brady nodded. "Couple of hours ago. Dan should be in soon. Went out for his last round shortly after I got here."

"Looks like a fine bunch of cattle this year, eh?" Rafe asked.

Pride floated through him as Brady grinned.

"I'm thinking we have more than enough saved for that extra special birthday present for JJ. I've already got things wrapped up so to speak." Brady replied.

Yes! They'd never told JJ that they now knew her birthday. Over the months they had asked her, but she had kept it a secret for some unknown reason. Thanks to Brady prodding his sister Jenna, they now knew the date.

Her birthday was just around the corner. He hoped she liked what they had gotten for her.

When Dan shuffled into camp, his ass was sore, his ears cold and his stomach was an empty hole.

Brady and Rafe were already here, so that meant dishes to do for him tonight.

Crap. But that was okay. It was their last night at this outdoor camp anyway. He hadn't realized how much he would miss JJ and now, with the roundup almost over, he missed her even more.

"Found a carcass out at the edge of one of the meadows," Dan said as he sat down on a tree stump that he was using for a chair. A satisfactory fatigue embraced him now that the drive was finally winding down. He accepted a steaming mug of soup and a thick slice of buttered bread from Rafe.

"Probably the pack of wolves that took down the cows in my section," Rafe replied.

"Yeah probably. It was an old kill, just like yours. Nothing left but bones. I just hope they don't head south and target the new crop of cattle," Dan said.

The other men grunted, but said nothing. Dan knew they were all too tired for small talk. Time to eat. Time to think.

It wasn't unusual to lose a few head of cattle every year due to the predators. But if things got worse, then they would have to hunt down the pack. For now though they would just take a wait and see approach.

Dan grinned at what Brady had confirmed with him earlier in the day when he'd met him on the trail, talking to someone on the sat phone. He wondered what JJ would say when she woke up on her birthday and discovered the items they had gotten for her.

All the hard work had been worth it if she loved her presents.

Dan's smile widened as he eagerly sipped his hot soup and chomped on the delicious bread.

EXCITEMENT WHIPPED through JJ as she gazed out her windshield to look at the rugged terrain below. It was her last hours of solo flying before the guys returned. Then her life would be back to the usual routine of caring for her men.

Bright sunshine splintered through the dark-blue clouds, casting a pretty glow on the colorful autumn tapestry below. Up ahead, on the lake, white swirls of waves indicated it would be a rough landing on the water. When she had left, the sky had been crystal clear and the winds calm, but the clouds and high winds as the weatherman had predicted on the net had since rolled in.

JJ wasn't nervous. Not much, anyway.

Over the past few days, she'd spent a couple of hours each day flying solo but she was still too uptight to try for her private pilot's license. As she prepared to land, she remembered the conversation earlier in the day she had had with Kaley while she had watched JJ do her pre-flight inspections.

"You know what? I think I will take you up on that offer that you made awhile back," JJ had said.

"What offer?" Kaley had asked with a frown.

"You had mentioned you would keep an eye out if a suitable plane came up for sale for me?"

"Oh, that. Sure. I remember. Well I haven't seen anything suitable yet but I am keeping my eyes open."

Disappointment hit JJ.

Oh, well. It was for the best anyway. She couldn't just up and buy a plane. They were expensive. Even the used ones that she had taken a look at online. But someday.

JJ put down the plane with no difficulty and tossed the rope to Kaley, who moored the plane to the dock. As JJ climbed out onto the pontoon with her knapsack in hand, she inhaled deeply. The autumn air smelled crisp and clean. If she didn't know any better, she would swear she could smell snow in the air. After a brief conversation with

Kaley about the next time they would meet up, they hugged and said their goodbyes and Kaley disappeared into the plane. A few minutes later, the white plane was soaring skyward and soon disappeared over the treetops. Excitement bubbled through her.

Yeah, maybe someday. Maybe she could have a plane of her very own.

Chapter Eight

RAFE DREAMED OF DARKNESS, pain and despair. He dreamed of howling gray wolves with black eyes and gleaming blood-red fangs. In his nightmare, he was back in the cabin after he had injured his leg.

Trapped, unmoving. Helpless. Freezing.

I'm going to die.

Rafe awoke in a cold sweat and sat straight up. As he did, pain exploded against his forehead and for a split second he had no idea what had just happened. Then he drew in a ragged breath as he spied the moonlight streaming in through one of the cabin windows. He cursed softly and remembered.

The day before had been long as they'd counted the cattle while loading them into the boxcars. A bitterly cold wind and snowflakes had swirled out of the gloomy steel-gray skies off and on all day long. When the train had pulled out, they had packed their gear and come here to the cabin. To the place that haunted his dreams.

Damn, this nightmare was frustrating. He rubbed a hand over the sore lump on his forehead and cursed softly.

He had taken a lower bunk and when he had sat up, he'd smashed his head on the wooden beam of the upper bunk. It appeared that the noise had not woken the guys. Soft snores whispered through the room.

Dan and Brady were sleeping soundly in nearby lower bunks. Probably dreaming about their upcoming reunion with JJ. Warmth bubbled up inside him as he thought about her. She was the sweetest, most beautiful woman in the world. He couldn't see himself with anyone but her.

Man, the scenario this time was so different than the last time he had been here. He should not be having such gloominess haunting his nights.

On a frustrated sigh, Rafe climbed out of his bunk. The room was still warm from the fire they had stoked in the wood stove when they'd gotten here, so he padded barefoot in his underwear to the nearest window. He gazed out and his breath caught at the moonlit landscape. The meadow surrounding the cabin was ablaze with sparkles of snowflakes. Not enough to accumulate, but just enough to make everything look pretty as the white flakes kissed the edges of the windowsill and the nearby pine boughs. He watched the scenery for awhile, knowing that if he went to bed he wouldn't sleep anymore.

Quietly he placed some more wood into the stove and set a pot of water on for the coffee. Then he donned his clothing. When he was dressed, the water was hot enough so he made some instant coffee. He'd drink it outside. He put on his hat and coat and grabbed his steaming mug and headed for the door. Just before he stepped outside, he hesitated as he spied the ax leaning up against a wall. A shiver shot through him.

His ax.

One of the guys had brought it in at some point. He gazed at the meager woodpile beside the cast-iron stove and remembered there hadn't been much emergency wood outside either. Maybe he should continue where he'd left off the last time he'd been here?

He reached out. His hand trembled as it hovered over the ax handle. The tool brought back the memories of the pain. The helplessness. The blade biting into his leg.

Defiance rolled over him and he grabbed the handle.

No more of this shit!

He was going to split some wood.

Damn his fears. And damn his panicky dreams. He was going to push through his demons just like JJ was pushing through hers.

Rafe quietly shut the door behind him. He left his coffee mug on the porch rail and stepped down the steps and went to where the chopping block awaited. Without hesitation he grabbed a cut log from the shoulder high pile, placed it on to a block and began his mission of casting out the demons that had invaded him and his dreams.

Satisfaction melted through him as the blade slashed the log right in half. Confidence soared as he kept chopping. By the time he was finished, his coat hung on the nearby railing, sweat blistered across his forehead and drenched his sweater and all his muscles ached like a son of a bitch.

Accomplishment made him smile as he stared at the waist-high pile of split logs.

Wow. He had cut like a man possessed and nothing bad had happened. Now he understood about that saying in pushing past your boundaries of fear. It felt exhilarating having chopped so much wood without anything bad happening again.

Liberating.

As he turned away from the pile to grab his coat, movement at the corner of his eye caught his attention. To his surprise Dan and Brady stood nearby with steaming coffee cups in their hands as they watched him.

Brady grinned and then lifted his coffee mug in greeting.

"Was wondering when you were going to finish," Dan called out.

"Ready to get moving? Looks like snow," Brady said and he nodded to the brightening gray sky. It was already dawn. He must have chopped for hours. A man possessed with demons.

Hopefully, he had cast those demons out for good.

"Let's bring in a couple of loads for whoever gets here in the spring," Rafe said.

Rafe grinned as Brady and Dan both groaned. But he knew they would help, because that's how they all worked. Like a well oiled team.

The two men placed their mugs on the nearby cabin windowsill and within seconds, they joined him, happily chatting about the long ride back to the ranch and to their sweet pot of gold waiting there.

JJ.

When Brady spied the ranch house the through the darkness, the buttery lights illuminating virtually all the windows on the first and second floors, happiness bubbled past his weariness. This was one welcome sight.

Man, was he sure glad to be home. One week and one day was just too long to be away from JJ. Next year, they would hire someone to do the chores around here and they could JJ along with them. He smiled at that thought. He knew all the guys would agree with him.

Brady pulled his four wheeler into the yard and waited for Rafe and Dan to join him. Seconds later, their machines roared into the yard where they all removed their helmets.

"Good to be back," Rafe said with a wink as he headed toward the door.

"Damn good," Dan agreed as he stepped in beside Rafe. Brady chuckled as he followed behind.

They had traveled the trails all day long, delayed a couple hours here and there as they chain-sawed through trees that had fallen across the trails due to the high winds. They had passed on supper to make up for lost time.

They were tired and they were hungry. In more ways than one.

Brady was surprised that JJ didn't meet them at the door. But the house smelled good as they went inside. It was a mingle of coffee, roast beef and...pumpkin pie? His mouth watered at the scent of cinnamon and allspice.

Man, the pie smelled exactly like the ones his mom used to bake. Remembering his late mother brought a mix of emotions. Sadness at her and his dad for not being alive and not being able to meet JJ. They would have loved her, he was sure about that. And happiness that he'd had such cool parents who had always supported him and his siblings, no matter what.

It had felt good to be in the embrace of such tremendous love and security. He still kept in touch with all his siblings, but they all led busy lives of their own. Especially Boone, who was just a year younger than he. They were so close in age and had been inseparable when they'd been kids.

Last he had talked to his brother Boone, he'd learned that he and a friend of his were talking about starting up their own ranch out west. One day he'd get up a reunion so they could all get together and catch up.

Brady shook away the thoughts of his siblings and wondered where JJ had gotten off to. Despite the late hour, he figured she would be waiting up and excited to see them. By the delicious cooking scents, she had to be around here somewhere.

As they entered the kitchen/dining room area, Brady gazed at Dan and Rafe. No sign of JJ. Dan frowned and Rafe shrugged his shoulders.

"Where is she?" Dan whispered.

Brady nodded toward the dining room table. It was laid out in fine form with a fancy white linen tablecloth and set with their finest dishes and cutlery. Red and white bottles of wine chilled in a container of ice. Coffee percolated in the machine.

On the table was a potato salad drenched in parsley and mustard. A rainbow-colored arrangement of vegetables from their garden and a casserole dish.

Brady watched Dan lift the lid of the dish. Steam curled upward. His mouth watered at the scents of onions and other spices.

"Roast beef with onions. Smells damned good," Dan said as he replaced the lid.

"There's three warm pumpkin pies in the oven. But the oven is off," Rafe said as he peered inside the stove.

Brady spied a small white wicker basket on the kitchen counter. The basket was decorated with a nice dark blue bow. A note dangled from the handle.

Brady snapped up the note.

JJ's feminine handwriting was neatly scrawled on the paper.

Welcome home, cowboys. What will it be? Roast beef dinner and pumpkin pie...or me?

Come and find me if you can and don't forget your cowboy hats.

Brady swore softly. Dan and Rafe crowded in around him. They swore quietly as they also read her taunt.

"Man, she sure knows how to welcome home her weary cowboys," Rafe said. Yet there wasn't an ounce of weariness in his voice.

Brady felt his batteries recharging too as Dan lifted three boxes of condoms from the basket. He tossed a small box to each of them and kept one to himself.

"There are cock rings in here too. One for each of us," Dan muttered.

"I'm already too hard to get one on," Rafe complained.

Brady swallowed as he peeked inside the basket. *Oh nice.* He lifted several tubes of massage oil. Different scents.

"Lavender. Vanilla. Strawberry. Lilac. Plum. Melon. And chocolate," he read out loud.

"Damn lot of massage oil. She must really have missed us," Rafe whispered with a grin.

"Where the heck did I leave my cowboy hat?" Dan suddenly asked. He grabbed the lilac-scented oil, clutched his box of condoms and headed for the stairs.

"I'm going to check for her upstairs," Rafe said as he grabbed a cock ring, a bottle of oil and ran to catch up to Dan.

"And I need a shower," Brady said beneath his breath.

Despite cleaning up in a creek a few hours ago, he figured he smelled too much of the outdoorsy scent. JJ would appreciate a clean-smelling cowboy. He grabbed a pack with the cock ring and the chocolate massage oil and headed for the nearest shower stall, just down the hall.

JJ sat quietly in the bedroom closet. She had just finished setting the table when she'd glanced out the kitchen window and spied the headlights piercing the darkness up the trail.

They were here! Late, but hey, better late than never. They had contacted her earlier in the afternoon via satellite phone letting her know they would delayed due to fallen trees on the trail and were forgoing supper to make up for lost time.

She had used the time to gather the ingredients for a late supper for them and to bake the pumpkin pies. Earlier in the day Jenna had called looking for Brady and JJ had told her she'd been about to scour the net for a decent pumpkin pie recipe when Jenna had told her she would send her her late mother's recipe, assuring her Brady and the guys would love it.

JJ had even undressed and worn nothing but a robe as she sang and cooked.

Then the roar of the ATVs had her scrambling for cover. In her note, she had told them they would have to find her. She'd planned on hiding in the upstairs guest room, but when she had gone down the back hallway to peek out the mudroom window, Brady, Dan and Rafe were already in the yard approaching the ranch house. She'd panicked and slipped into the first available room. The office.

Knowing there was a good chance one of them would walk right in here and find her, JJ dove into the closet.

As she waited, JJ gazed around the dark interior. For a few harrowing seconds, the familiar uneasiness of the walls closing in on her breathed a warning of anxiety. But she quickly turned her thoughts away from those fears of being locked in. Moved her thoughts of listening to her stepfather beating her mother on the other side of the closet door. Killing her.

Shivers crawled through her and she forced herself to calm her rapid breathing. She knew she had to nip this anxiety in the bud before it snowballed into something she could not control.

The memory cannot hurt me. I will not let this feeling of fear ruin my evening. My thoughts cannot hurt me. Think of something else. Something pleasant.

JJ smiled and nodded.

Loving her cowboys. Brady. Dan. Rafe. The three men held her heart captive and her body hostage to the pleasures they gave her so freely.

Oh boy, she needed to see their sweet faces. Impatience made JJ crack open the closet door and she inhaled the fresh air sifting inside.

Silence. Where had they gone? Upstairs? Looking for her.

A swishing sound came from somewhere nearby. The shower? One of the guys was taking a shower down here?

Hmm, what a delicious place to hide out while the other two men searched for her. Heat whipped through her as she spied Brady's black cowboy hat hanging on a hook at the back of the office door. She wondered who she would find in the shower.

She grabbed the hat and plopped it onto her head, then tiptoed out of the office, and into the hall.

She smiled as she heard two sets of footsteps clomping around upstairs.

A moment later, she slipped into the steamy, warm bathroom. Clothes lay rumpled on top of the counter. She recognized Brady's green sweater and plaid flannel shirt. A shadow moved behind the frosted glass shower door. She spied the chocolate massage oil on the counter. The box of condoms.

Perfect!

In a flash, she'd removed her robe and quickly massaged the tingling edible chocolate oil over her breasts, belly and between her thighs. She grabbed a condom from the box, ripped off the foil and placed the protection between her teeth, careful to not clamp down on the thin barrier.

Then she stopped. A hole in the condom could produce a baby.

JJ sucked in a sharp breath at that thought.

A family that you always wanted is right here waiting for you.

A baby with Brady.

Oh, wow. She had toyed with the idea that one day a condom would break and she might get pregnant. She had thought about having babies. Raising them here. Homeschooling them.

Three kids. Three different fathers.

She smiled as she imagined having beautiful children, each one with their father's features. She would treat them as gently as her mother had treated her. With a guiding hand. No criticism. No yelling or screaming.

She couldn't think of any other men who she would want to father her children. The idea of making babies actually aroused her. How weird was that? Or maybe it was erotic? JJ reached out, and slowly slid open the glass door.

The lavender soap Brady was using smelled just like JJ, he thought as he faced the wall and allowed the jets of hot water to pummel his face while he rubbed soap into his tense shoulder muscles. He had just stepped into the shower and he already couldn't wait to get out and find her.

Man, what had possessed him into taking a shower? The guys had probably already found her and were tying her to her bed, getting ready to take turns with her. He wanted to see her so bad, his cock was so intense, he hadn't thought the cock ring would even fit. But after some quick maneuvering, the ring now tortured the base of his shaft. Tortured in a good way.

As he soaked his chest, he thought about how delicious JJ would look, her wrists bound, her legs spread-eagled. Her body would quiver with anticipation as he climbed onto the bed, over her and then thrust into her.

His breaths quickened and to his surprise he groaned out loud. The sound was guttural. Primal. Animalistic.

He stepped back and allowed the water to pummel his chest. Something touched his ass cheek. It was a light feathery touch that made him wonder if maybe a fly had climbed into the shower with him?

That would be a first.

Suddenly, a brush whispered over his left shoulder. He gazed down and smiled as he spied fingers.

Sneaky woman.

In a flash, he turned and had her backed up against the back of the small shower stall.

Damn, she looked cute wearing his black cowboy hat. The look of surprise in her sparkling eyes had him excited and the black condom between her lips had his shaft reacting big time.

The emotions whipping through JJ just about killed her. She was surprised at how fast Brady had moved, his quick subduing of her had her holding her breath and dropping the condom from her lips.

Impressive instincts. Great father material.

The dark need sparkling in his eyes had her reaching up and spearing her fingers through his wet hair. She stood on her tiptoes, her lips parting as she angled her head toward his.

Wow, he looked good. He hadn't shaved today, so a dark black stubble caressed his cheeks and chin.

Such a sexy man. All hers. Her man.

He moved closer and his hot body heat caressed her flesh. JJ kissed him and her world rocked. He braced his arms on both sides of her shoulders, and he kissed her back so hard that her thoughts spun away and her instincts took over.

Brady's thick, hot cockhead massaged her sensitive clit, making her moan at the burst of pleasure. His lips parted hers, pushed inside and stroked her tongue like a long-lost lover. She did not know how long he kissed her and she vaguely remembered pulling away from him. She found herself staring at him. Studying every crevice of his face, his gorgeous mouth. Suddenly his deep voice whispered through her senses.

"What is it, JJ? Why are you looking at me like this? What do you want, sweetness?"

Suddenly she just wanted to beg. To tell him what she knew deep in her heart. That she had never been so sure of anything in her life.

"Give me a baby, Brady."

She wasn't sure if he had heard her because he didn't even blink. His face appeared blank as he stared at her.

Shock, maybe? Did he think she was crazy? Maybe she was. But it felt right to have Brady as the father of her first child.

"Well, this is unexpected," he muttered. He held her gaze. Seemed to be studying her. Maybe trying to figure out if it was a good idea or not?

For a split second, she thought he might say no, but then the tips of lips lifted into a tummy-clenching smile.

"A baby is a permanent bond. Are you sure?" he asked. There was an erotic edge to his voice.

JJ nodded as raw emotions welled up from her chest. Tears prickled her eyes. His arms dropped away from her sides and she inhaled sharply as he cupped her breasts. Held them as if they were precious cargo.

"Our baby suckling here," he said. There was awe in his voice.

"Hold me. Fuck a baby into me."

Before she even finished her words, Brady's lips touched hers. Then they melted hot and tickling and with utter possession over hers.

He kissed her rough and then soft and everything in between. Kissed her until her mouth tingled and her toes curled.

When he pulled away, JJ felt so drugged and giddy, she could barely stand.

His eyes were dark and lusty. His lips red as he dropped his gaze to her breasts.

"How can I refuse chocolate-covered breasts?" he muttered thickly.

She cried out as he lowered his head and sucked a nipple into his mouth. Stimulating arousal zinged through her as he nibbled, sucked and slurped. His hands uncupped her and then trailed down over her belly. His hand splayed over her abdomen.

"Our baby growing inside of you. The idea of it makes me so hot for you, I can barely stand it."

Me too!

JJ widened her stance and one of Brady's hands dipped between her quivering thighs. Fingers parted her chocolate-oiled folds and she arched as a thumb massaged her clit with confident strokes.

His mouth moved over to her other breast. He sucked on her nipple and made incredible sensations dance through her.

Suddenly, shadows appeared on the other side of the frosted glass door. At first she thought she imagined them, but then the door slid open.

Dan and Rafe stood there.

Laughter and lust twinkled in their eyes as they watched Brady. Then their gazes captured JJ's.

"So, this is where you're hiding," Dan chuckled.

Rafe nodded. He was biting his lower lip. He appeared eager and so sexy with a five o'clock shadow on his face.

"I am going to give JJ a baby," Brady suddenly said.

She hadn't even realized that he'd stopped sucking her nipples. They tingled with fire, compliments of the chocolate massage oil. He continued massaging her clit, keeping her on the edge. Making her needy. Wanting.

She tried to read the guys' faces for a reaction. But there was none to what Brady had just said. No jealousy. But she did read willing acceptance.

"What do you need us to do?" Rafe asked.

"I'm to wear no condoms from here on out," Brady said around her nipple. His voice sounded guttural. Territorial.

Dan and Rafe nodded. That Dan and Rafe would continue with protection went unsaid. But she knew they understood Brady's meaning.

JJ sucked in a breath as two of Brady's fingers entered her. Her need for release increased and she clamped her thighs around his hand. Mindlessly she began to gyrate, but Brady withdrew and chuckled.

"Not yet, baby. You're nice and wet. Wouldn't want that to go to waste."

He turned to the guys.

"Get the bed ready across the hall. I want her tied down when I take her. We'll be there in a minute."

Dan and Rafe moved quickly. Within a blink of an eye, they were gone.

JJ's pussy clenched as Brady stared into her eyes. He was serious. Stern.

"Once we start, there is no going back. Are you sure about this?" he said as he cupped her chin with one hand.

JJ nodded jerkily, her entire body tensing as she became full of awareness.

"We are going to tie you down, baby. All three of us inside you. But only me inside your pussy." Brady said.

His words made her cream.

"Don't say I didn't warn you, sweetness," he growled.

He let go of her chin and turned off the water. In a flash, she was in his arms. Both of them were dripping wet as he carried her out of the shower stall, and a moment later she was in the bedroom across the hall.

The room was dimly lit with one small lamp on a corner table.

This was where it had all begun. In this room. She had just come to the ranch a little under a year ago. She'd gotten into a wine supply on the bush plane that had brought her here. She'd been trying to drown her anxieties at being on a plane. The walls closing in.

She'd made herself drunk and the anxiety meds she'd been prescribed had made the booze that much more potent. When they'd landed on the ice, she'd sat on her suitcases and watched the big man walk down to the lake where she sat. Something exciting had raged through her. After he had led her to the ranch house, he'd been upset and gruff with her, trying to ply her with coffee to sober her up.

He had brought her in here. It was that night she had discovered her fetish for cowboy hats. Had insisted he wear one.

Now Dan and Rafe stood beside the bed, both wearing their cowboy hats. They stroked their long, engorged cocks and JJ shivered as she spied the ropes tied to each of the posts of the bed. Attached to the end of each rope were two leather, fur-lined cuffs, instead of one.

Curiosity raged. What were they up to with two cuffs? She'd find out soon enough.

Having three men surrounding her made the blood pound wildly through her bloodstream. She was already highly tuned from Brady tending to her in the shower, but now gazing at the cuffs and seeing Dan and Rafe's engorged shafts, JJ felt like she might explode from this eroticism.

"Rafe, lie on the bed. Face up," Brady growled as he set her on her feet.

Rafe moved quickly and JJ watched as he climbed onto the bed. Rafe's movements were confident, his body sleek, muscular and tan.

He lay on his back, his cock rigid as a pole. His eyes were heavy-lidded as he reached onto the night table and grabbed a condom.

A few seconds later, he was sheathed and then he continued to stroke his shaft, watching her with a predatory gaze that sent awareness shooting through her.

"Lube her ass," Brady instructed Dan and then Brady took her into his arms.

"Your last chance, baby. From here on out, we're in it for the long haul."

"I'm not changing my mind," she whispered.

His eyes darkened and his head lowered. He kissed her so deeply she saw stars.

Behind her, Dan smoothed a soft towel along her arms, her back and then down her legs, drying off the excess water from the shower. He caressed her ass with the towel and then the cloth was gone. She trembled when the slurp of lube followed. A moment later, Dan pressed a lubed finger against her protesting sphincter.

JJ creamed and arched against Brady as Dan pushed the lube into her and then withdrew. Brady's cockhead nudged against her clit, erupting heat and shuddering sensations. Need swiftly uncoiled deep inside JJ's belly. She cried into Brady's mouth as Dan slid two lubed fingers into her ass. She knew Dan would prepare her well because Rafe's cock was big and Dan didn't want her hurt.

He used his fingers to manipulate her muscles with the gel until they relaxed.

Brady's hands smoothed over her lower belly, his touches making her groan and press harder against Brady. She kissed him rougher as she became desperate for more pleasure. But his tongue continued to patiently stroke hers until she became heady and her cream of desire dripped from her.

"She's prepared." Dan's voice was guttural as he withdrew his fingers from her ass.

Brady broke the kiss and the two of them breathed heavily, their cheeks pressed together.

"Ready?" Brady asked. She detected the eagerness in his voice. Brady was fully committed, JJ had no doubt.

She would never turn back from making a baby with Brady. Never. Then, sometime in the future, she would decide on who would father her next baby.

Rafe or Dan. Or maybe she would play Russian roulette with them and they'd guess who the father would be.

JJ grinned inwardly. She loved her unorthodox ideas of lovemaking and making babies. She had to be either completely mad or had entered a sensual world most women had no idea could exist.

"Up on the bed, sweetness. Impale your ass on Rafe. Dan will take your mouth," Brady said with a firmness that turned her on. She liked this dominant side of him. No arguments, just brisk sexy orders.

As she climbed onto the bed beside Rafe, he caught her gaze and held it. His look was ultra-dark and sensual.

"We'll all be bonded together after this, JJ," he whispered. Full and utter approval sparkled in his eyes.

"It will be a beautiful bond. A beautiful baby."

"Yes, the most beautiful baby," she agreed. She loved that Rafe was so accepting of her decision and that he wanted to be a part of creating her baby in this way.

"Hop on baby girl, let's go for a wild ride," Rafe instructed as he held the base of his cock with both his hands.

Her pussy clenched as Brady helped her squat over Rafe's torso. Then Dan was at her other side, cradling her ass with his strong hands, helping her into position.

She keened as the hot tip of Rafe's condom-covered shaft nudged against her hole. She squatted some more, lowering herself slowly. She felt every inch of his heated length as it slid into her. Fire raced through her as she clenched around the thick intrusion.

When she was fully impaled, Dan and Brady helped her to lie down with her back on Rafe, who had spread eagled his legs. They placed her legs upon Rafe's legs and as the cuffs were secured around both herself and Rafe, she understood that the cuffs would hold her in place with Rafe. It was such an erotic idea that it almost drove her crazy.

Quickly Dan led Rafe's left arm up and secured his wrist with the cuff and then brought her arm right on top of Rafe's arm securing her wrist with the cuff attached to Rafe's. Brady did the same to Rafe's and her other arm.

Hot, pulsing lust whipped through JJ. This was an unusual position for her to be in, but incredibly erotic being impaled and cuffed to Rafe and also using him as her mattress. His body heat burned through her flesh and his cock throbbed deep inside her ass. The muscles of his hard, lean body flexed beneath her and his hot breaths caressed her right cheek.

His heart thudded against the left side of her back, in sync with her beats, a sign that their hearts were aligned and bonded. The idea was so endearing.

"You feel nice and snug, JJ. Absolutely perfect," Rafe growled against her ear.

JJ wished she could talk, but her gaze was magnetized to Dan now as he climbed over her upper half. His shaft was long and engorged as he angled it toward her lips.

"Open up, sweetie," Dan coaxed.

She did as he instructed, and his condom-sheathed shaft slipped into her mouth. His cock jerked and Dan hissed his approval. His flesh stretched her lips, and he pushed into her until he almost touched the back of her throat. He curled the fingers of one hand up near the base, a guide that indicated he should not go farther than his fingers. Then he pulled out and slid into her slowly again, creating a tingling friction against her lips.

"Suck me, baby. Suck me hard. Just knowing that we're all going to be making a baby is making me crazy for you," he growled and grinned down at her. His eyes sparkled and his cowboy hat was set off center on his head, making him look so cute.

She tightened her lips on him as he began a deep, erotic pistoning.

Need tormented her at having Rafe and Dan inside of her. She needed Brady too.

As if sensing what she was thinking, she felt the mattress dip in the middle of her legs. Movement followed between her thighs.

Brady.

Anticipation made her hollow her cheeks and suck harder on Dan. Her thighs tightened as Brady's warm breath teased her sensitized clit. Erotic shudders made her moan around Dan's shaft and instinctively she gyrated her hips.

Beneath her, Rafe groaned as her anal muscles clenched around him. It was like a chain reaction. Whatever she movement she did, it affected one of the guys. It was pretty cool.

JJ tensed as Brady's hands slid along the insides of her thighs, making them quiver.

Oh, his touch feels so wonderful.

She bucked and pulled at her restrained hands and legs as Brady's teeth nipped at her pussy lips. Then he sucked and pulled on her labia until the pleasure pain became almost unbearable. Beneath her, Rafe moaned and gyrated his hips, creating a wild pressure deep inside her ass as his cock flexed and throbbed.

Blood pounded through her as Brady let go of her labia and fused his hot mouth over her shuddering pussy. His tongue lashed her clit like a whip, stirring up a mirage of trembles and pleasure.

This is crazy good!

She lost track of time and vanished inside a vortex of need as the three men played and teased and destroyed her, turning her into their sexual play toy. Every inch of her flesh sizzled with fire and her senses became fine tuned to their groans and grunts.

She became one with them.

JJ sucked harder on Dan's shaft, giving him the pleasure he needed. His pistoning became faster and erratic, and suddenly his cock pulsed and jerked uncontrollably between her lips. She sucked and slurped on his quivering flesh, enjoying Dan's gasps as he neared his orgasm. Then he was there. He jerked once. Twice. Three times. His shouts echoing through the bedroom as he came into his condom.

Soon, all too soon, he was pulling out of her mouth.

Then Brady moved away from her pussy and she watched him, helpless and bound, as he climbed over her. Perspiration blossomed over her as his eyes met hers. His pupils were dilated and black as sin and filled with intent. He appeared so aroused that she wasn't even sure if Brady was even Brady.

His cock looked angry, hard and ultra-thick.

Awareness tightened everything inside of JJ.

He looked wild, his teeth bared. The large muscles in his arms bulged as he moved into position over top of both herself and Rafe. She blinked up at him and eagerly awaited him as he lowered his body.

She was so taut she knew the instant he touched her she would come apart.

And she did.

Without warning, he drove into her vagina, slamming his hips against hers, sending her straight into the pleasure storm. JJ convulsed into a myriad of shudders. Explosions tore through her. Every inch of her tightened and trembled. Every nerve ending sparked and ignited.

Brady withdrew and plunged into her again. Immediately he set up a steady, firm pistoning. He went so deep inside of her, she swore he touched places no man had ever touched.

JJ writhed and bucked, her body uncontrollable. From somewhere she heard Rafe shout. Heard Brady hiss and moan as he kept up the hard, driving tempo.

The orgasm crashed through her, taking her mind and her body, leaving her trembling and moaning. When the shudders ebbed, Brady teased her some more. His plunges harder and faster and she felt the burn of another climax form.

Her pussy felt ultra-swollen, her clit so aroused and sensitive that as Brady thrust against her again and again, she could barely comprehend the ecstasy. His mouth fused over hers and he kissed her so hard that electric tingles bruised her lips.

JJ exploded again. This time with a deeper intensity. A harder orgasm. Violent pleasure cocooned her and carried her into an existence of electric colors, glittering space and mind-numbing desire. Deep into an existence where agony and wonder met. Into a world she had never been to. A world she wanted to explore forever.

Rafe swore JJ had never made such erotic, animalist noises before during their lovemaking sessions. The pleasure sounds were beautiful. Like delicate music. The sexy noises made love to his senses and the harsh pummelling of Brady's thrusts as he slammed into JJ over and over again created such a sensual friction that bursts of pleasure wrapped tightly around him and just wouldn't let go. Heat melted his self-control and he came on a shout.

Jolts of electricity circled the entire length of his shaft. It squeezed his tender flesh like a vise and shot sparks deep into his belly and straight into his very core. The pleasure was so intense it was painful and mind-splintering.

He shook and squirmed as he flew along the currents of pleasure. The kaleidoscope of shivers embraced him and dragged him under. He was sinking. Drowning in love and pleasure and agony.

Damn, he sure was glad he had survived that accident to experience this unbelievable experience. Damned glad.

Dan watched the three bodies writhing together on the bed. The scene appeared so erotic that he couldn't help but stroke his shaft back to life again. Man, he was so thankful to have JJ in his life. So thankful for everything he had right now.

As Dan listened to JJ's whimpers and moans, he quickly tensed and then came apart again, groaning as wicked blades of pleasure shocked through him like a sweet-edged knife.

Making a baby was going to be so much fun.

Chapter Nine

BRADY WAS LOST INSIDE of JJ. He pushed into her over and over again. Every thrust brought her closer to yet another climax. Each of her orgasms were more intense than the one before. Each one drove him closer to losing his self-control.

She had thrown him a curve tonight when she'd asked him to make her pregnant. The thought had crossed his mind many times over the past weeks and months, but it had always been a "what if the condom broke and she got pregnant" kind of thing. But he'd never taken the idea ultra-seriously until he'd seen the intense way she'd been exploring his face in the shower.

He'd never seen such a look of love shining in her eyes before. It had been as if she'd been dipped into a world of wonder. A world he wanted to join her in. Making a baby was a journey he had until now only dreamed about. He wanted only the best for JJ. He loved her. Loved her so damned much it hurt.

A baby will be nice.

He would give her what she wanted, and so much more. As JJ flew into another orgasm, her pussy muscles squeezed his shaft so snug that Brady finally lost it.

His self-control vanished and took him right along with it as he plunged so far into her he swore even his mind was orgasming inside the killing pleasure.

He kissed her like a man possessed, absorbing her moans into his very being. He branded her with his cock, thrusting so deep that he melded their bodies together and joined her spirit.

Yeah, they would make a baby together. And many more if he got his way.

Many, many more.

JJ SLEPT THE DEEPEST she had ever slept in her life. The darkness was silent, soothing, healing. Through the layers of sleep, she slowly moved upward. Finally voices appeared within her realm.

Rafe. Dan. Brady.

She smiled as she listened to them. She figured they were in the kitchen. They seemed happy, excited. She didn't know what they were saying, but she could tell in their voices that whatever was happening was something big.

She opened her eyes. Sunshine streamed in through the bedroom windows. Bright and beautiful sunlight. It made her so happy.

It was a perfect day to begin a new life. She reached down and smoothed a hand over her belly. Her pussy throbbed and her ass clenched as she remembered the three men making love to her last night.

It hadn't been sex. It had been pure love.

Brady loved her. She had felt it. Dan and Rafe loved her too. She knew it. Sensed it in the men's behavior whenever they were around her. How they watched her move. How they laughed with her and sweetly teased her.

JJ frowned as she suddenly noticed the guys had fallen silent. What were they up to?

The bliss of after lovemaking broke as she gazed at the nearby clock. Nine fifteen a.m.? She blinked in shock.

Had the batteries in the clock died?

No, woman. Give your head a shake.

Sunshine streamed in through the windows. It was after nine. She never slept in this late! Why hadn't the guys woken her? She'd wanted to help them unpack from their cattle drive and make them a delicious, healthy breakfast.

Oh shoot, she should have put all the food away into the fridge last night. Everything might have spoiled. No, wait a minute. She vaguely remembered some time in the middle of the night one of the guys saying they had put everything into the fridge.

But still. She should have been up and serving them at six a.m.. This was ranch living. People didn't take days off and lounge around in bed. Cows had to be tended. Fences had to be fixed. Trails cleared. The rest of the garden had to be harvested and stored.

Guilt wrapped around her. There was so much to do and here she was lying in bed. She was about to push aside the warm comforters when the bedroom door suddenly burst inward.

Brady stood there with a huge grin on his face. Rafe and Dan were crowding in right behind him.

"Happy birthday, baby," Brady shouted.

Surprise rocked her. Her birthday? She did a quick mental calculation and realized that yes, today was her birthday.

She dropped her gaze and spied the the large cake in Brady's hands. The cake was in the shape of a cowboy hat. Bright pink candles with small flickering flames stuck out of the snow-white icing.

JJ blinked as disbelief flooded her.

She had stopped celebrating her birthday when her mom died. It had been too painful to rejoice so she had tried hard to forget about it. She'd forgotten entirely that today was her birthday and now as they stood here excited to celebrate, she was surprised she didn't feel sad. Instead, she wanted to rejoice with them!

Gosh, they looked so different from last night. They were all clean-shaven and all three of them wore their cowboy hats. They were also dressed in formal attire. Each wore a black suit and a colorful tie. Each pressed jacket had a red rose pinned to the breast pocket.

JJ couldn't help but laugh as her heart burst with so much love for them.

"Oh my gosh. You guys look so gorgeous," she whispered.

"Don't sound so surprised, beautiful. We do look pretty dashing when we clean ourselves up, if I do say so myself," Brady said with a grin.

"We bring you cake and all you do is look at our clothes?" Dan chuckled as the three men strolled into the bedroom.

"Typical woman," Rafe muttered with a shake of his head.

"Blow out your candles, baby doll. Make a wish. But don't tell us or it won't come true," Brady said. His white teeth flashed against his tanned face.

Okay, they are up to something. She sensed it. Could read it in their body language. Their too-bright smiles. A little anxiousness in their quick movements.

"Come on, JJ, blow out those candles," Rafe urged.

She clutched the comforters over her breasts as she struggled into a seated position. Her ass and pussy throbbed pleasantly with her every movement and it reminded her once again of what had happened between the four of them last night. Tying her down to the bed and fucking her senseless had only been the beginning. Afterward, they'd released her from the ropes and each man had taken turns with her again.

But only Brady had taken her vaginally and without a condom. Dan and Rafe had taken her in the ass.

She shivered sweetly as her butt clenched over empty air. She wanted all of them taking her again. But it would have to be later. They needed to get work done before playtime came around again. Besides, she needed to feed them.

She smiled as she read the words scrawled in brown over the white icing; *Happy Birthday, JJ.*

She leaned closer, took a deep breath and blew.

The flames flickered and all of the candles went out. She made her wish. Actually two wishes. Call her selfish, but yeah, two wishes.

"Good job sweetheart. Now get dressed and meet us out on the front porch. We've got something to show you."

Before she could question them as to what they were up too, the three men chatted happily as they rushed out of the room with that cake.

"I'll put the coffee on," Rafe said as he entered the hall.

"I'll set the table," she heard Brady reply.

"I'll eat the cake," Dan stated. All three men laughed.

Warmth and the sweetest happiness melted through JJ.

Goodness. They had better not have spent any money on her or she would kill them. She whipped aside the comforters and padded across the hall for a quick shower.

JJ SWORE SOFTLY BENEATH her breath after she showered and got dressed in record time. She'd grabbed a pair of freshly laundered jeans and a slightly wrinkled blue blouse from the basket of the clothing she had left in the mudroom yesterday.

When she entered the kitchen, it was empty. The scent of coffee hung in the air but there was no sign of the cake or the coffee. And the coffee machine was missing!

Then she remembered she was supposed to meet them on the porch.

Weird, because there was nowhere for them to eat outside, unless they had set up a picnic blanket out in the yard? Wasn't it too cold to be outside?

She headed back down the hallway to the mudroom and found her winter jacket and her warm wool hat.

How cool! Birthday cake for breakfast, outdoors. She could handle that. She pushed open the side door and stepped onto the wraparound porch. A brisk autumn air slapped against her face and she was glad she'd put on her coat and hat.

Huh. It was very quiet out here. No one was around. Had she remembered wrong? She stepped around to the front of the house and froze.

Dan and Rafe were seated at a gorgeous knotty pine picnic table she had never seen before. The table was decked out with an abundance of fruit and her birthday cake was there too. Pancakes and bacon sizzled on a griddle. Brady stood at the far end of the table where he scrambled eggs on a propane camp cook stove and they had even brought out the coffee machine.

"You like, JJ? It's a picnic table made especially for you. We harvested some trees and cut the wood in the sawmill and put the furniture together awhile back. We were sure you would find it, even after we'd hidden them in the vehicle shed and covered everything beneath a tarp. Plus..." Dan said and pointed to an area farther down the porch where a canopied knotty pine swing had been placed.

JJ's breath caught at the beautiful yellow-and-blue floral pattern on the material and the cushioned seats.

"We made the swing too. We hope you like the material," Dan said.

"During downtime, you can come out here and relax on your swing and watch the sunset," Rafe said.

"Every Saturday morning we will serve you breakfast out here on the picnic table, sweetness," Brady added as he kept scrambling the eggs.

Tears welled up in JJ's eyes. This was so unbelievable. No one had made her anything in her life.

"What have you guys done? How could I not catch on to what you were up to?" JJ asked as she walked over to the swing. She sat down on the plush cushion and moved back and forth on the swing. It rocked her gently. It would be perfect for rocking a baby to sleep too.

Mentally, she calculated nine months ahead. End of July. Perfect weather.

"Do you think she likes it?" Brady asked as he gazed at JJ.

"I think she likes it," Dan replied.

"I think she more than likes it," Rafe added.

He patted the seat beside him on the table bench where he sat.

"Come. Sit. Eat breakfast. We have one more surprise for you, but we'll get to that later."

"Another surprise? You three have totally freaked me out for the rest of my life," JJ said as she reluctantly got off the comfortable swing. She would inspect their workmanship later. But, wow, the swing was a beauty and so was the picnic table.

She sat down beside Rafe and before long, the guys were telling her all about their week on the cattle drive and how they were going to build a nice little cabin near the railroad. JJ was already imagining what kind of material she would buy to make the curtains.

JJ swore that eating outdoors made the food taste so good, and before long they were all nursing their third cups of coffee and slices of cake. The men's voices turned softer as conversation went to having a baby in the ranch house.

"We're going to have to build outward and upward," Brady said as he gazed toward the back area of the house.

"I was thinking the same thing," Rafe replied.

Brady nodded. "We could add two bedrooms upstairs for the kids. Girls in one room. Boys in another room. And on the ground floor a nice big playroom for them. When we were growing up I can't tell you how cool it was to share a bedroom with a couple of my brothers. Our house was small, but it was full of love."

JJ's heart melted at Brady's words.

"Yeah, it was kind of cool having a bunch of foster brothers and sisters. As you know, my mom and dad adopted two boys and two girls in addition to all the foster kids, and then I came as a big surprise because they'd been told they couldn't have kids because of my dad's low sperm count. But yeah, it was nice having a full house," Rafe added.

"I had my own room. But having two sisters was kind of cool, when they weren't bugging me. I always wished I could have had a brother or two to share my room with," Dan said with a grin.

JJ swallowed the last of her coffee and set her mug down.

"And exactly how many children are we planning to pack into this house?" she asked.

All three men looked at her. Heated lust filled their eyes.

"Enough to fill the house," Dan replied.

"More than enough," Rafe said with a wink.

"As many as you want, baby," Brady said.

Suddenly Brady stood and held out his hand to her. She slipped her palm against his and he helped her from the picnic table.

"We're going to blindfold you, sweetheart," Rafe said from right behind her.

"This is going to be the biggest surprise. It will blow your mind." Dan produced a rectangle piece of material that matched that on the canopy swing. He folded the material and then placed it over her eyes, knotting the blindfold behind her head.

She wasn't sure she could handle another surprise, she thought, as they held her by her elbows and led her down the ranch steps. Mentally, she tried to figure out where they were taking her. But she quickly got turned around and had no clue.

They walked a few minutes, the conversation about babies continuing.

"I think we should have three girls and three boys," Rafe said.

Oh my goodness.

"Or maybe all girls. I would want them to look as beautiful as JJ and just as smart," Brady said with a softness in his voice that made JJ believe he was serious.

"Or maybe all boys," Dan replied.

A house full of guys. JJ almost laughed. She would be the only female in a house full of men. How would she find her sons suitable women to marry when the nearest neighbor was a hundred kilometers away? How would she find her daughters suitable men to marry when no men existed nearby?

The crashing of waves onto the shore made her realize they were leading her to the lake.

Hmm, perhaps they'd made an extra Adirondack chair for the dock? They only had three chairs. Yeah, that was it. She would act surprised. She wouldn't tell them she had guessed.

She smiled as they slowed.

"Ready for your surprise, JJ?" Dan asked.

"You guys really shouldn't have gone to so much trouble for me," JJ gushed. But she really was pleased with everything.

"No trouble, sweetheart. Never any trouble where you are concerned," Brady growled in a deep voice.

"You are our top priority, baby. You take care of us. We wouldn't be where we are if you weren't taking such good care of us," Rafe said softly.

"And that's why we got you this," Brady said.

The blindfold was removed and JJ blinked as the dock rolled into focus. She looked farther up the dock expecting to see the extra Adirondack chair, but instead she saw something bigger.

Much, much bigger.

"Oh my gosh," JJ whispered. She couldn't believe what she was looking at.

And that is why we got you this.

"You like?" Rafe asked from right beside her.

Pinch me, please. This cannot be happening.

Moored at the far end of the dock was a white bush plane, pontoons and all. Not just any white plane, but Kaley's plane. They must have rented it. Maybe they wanted her to take them up flying?

Oh, they were going to be so disappointed.

"I can't take you up. I don't have my license yet."

She expected to see their happy faces fall into frowns. But they didn't. They were putting on such a brave face.

She felt so bad.

"No, we bought it. For you. For the ranch. Your suggestion made sense," Dan said.

"And we've been talking to Kaley via the Internet over the past weeks. She told us that you fly like a pro. That you are like a duck to water. She brought the plane in really early this morning with Blue bringing her plane along too so she could give Kaley a ride back. We didn't tell them it was your birthday present and that today was your birthday or they would have stayed and given you well wishes. We wanted you all to ourselves today. We kept hoping you wouldn't wake up hearing two planes out on the lake. But you were dead to the world every time we looked in on you," Rafe said. He winked and then headed toward the plane and Dan chuckled as he followed.

"How do you like your new toy?" Brady asked. His arm slipped around her waist and he pulled her against his hard warm body.

This is crazy.

"Brady, it's not a toy. It's too expensive," she whispered. She couldn't take her eyes off the plane. Her plane? Their plane? It glistened in the early morning sunlight. It looked so sharp against the dark-blue lake.

I have to be dreaming.

Brady chuckled.

"Kaley bought another plane. Hers was up for sale, but we asked her not to tell you," Brady squeezed her even tighter.

"You like?" he asked, giving her a squeeze.

This is insane.

She nodded jerkily.

"Good." He let go of her.

"I'm going down to check it out. Coming to show us around inside?"

"Just give me a minute." Her voice was barely above a whisper.

His grin widened, satisfaction etched his face. Then he turned and stomped along the wide dock to join Rafe and Dan who had both just hopped onto the pontoon and were climbing into the plane.

They were trusting her with a plane. They had bought a plane.

Wow. She'd had no idea that one of her dreams would come true so quickly. Her hands slipped down and settled over her belly.

She had no doubt that her other wish would soon be growing inside of her.

JJ shook her head, not believing how her luck had turned in just one year. She took a step forward and then another.

Up ahead was her future.

Brady. Rafe. Dan. A baby. Her plane.

How in the world could her life get any better? She had everything. For the first time in a long time she didn't have that inner restlessness of wanting something else, because now she had it all.

Her cowboys were loving her and she was loving her cowboys.

Spunky Girl Publishing Mini Catalog

~ Jan Springer ~ Erotic Romance ~

Cowboys For Christmas
Cowboys Online 1 ~ Moose Ranch
Jan Springer
A Canadian Contemporary Ménage Romance m/f/m/m Series

Jennifer Jane (JJ) Watson has spent the past ten Christmases in a maximum-security prison.

The last thing she expects is to get early parole, along with a job on a remote Canadian cattle ranch serving Christmas holiday dinners to three of the sexiest cowboys she's ever met!

Rafe, Brady and Dan thought they were getting a couple of male ex-cons to help out around their secluded ranch, but instead they get an attractive and very appealing female.

In the snowbound wilds of Northern Ontario, female companionship is rare.

It's a good thing the three men like to share...

They're dominating, sexy-as-sin and they fill JJ with the hottest ménage fantasies she's ever had. Suddenly she's craving cowboys for Christmas and wishing for something she knows she can never have...a happily ever after.

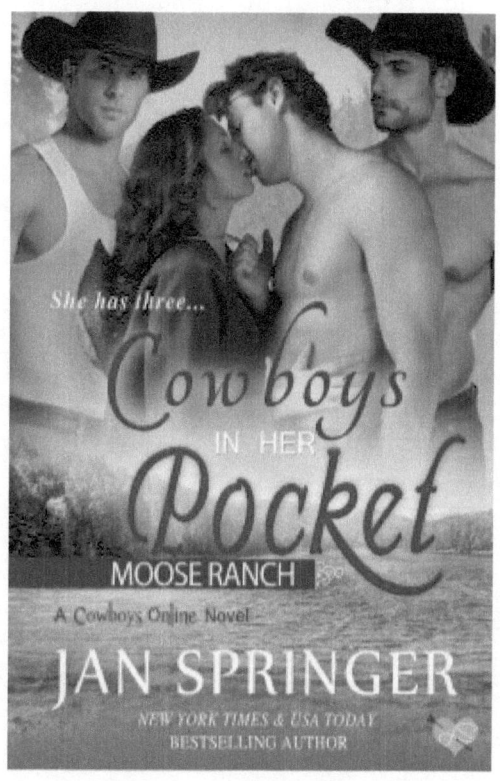

Cowboys In Her Pocket
Cowboys Online 2 ~ Moose Ranch
Jan Springer

After spending ten years in a maximum-security prison Jennifer Jane (JJ)
Watson got early parole and a job on a remote Canadian cattle ranch
playing housekeeper to three of the sexiest cowboys she's ever met...
Spring has finally arrived at Moose Ranch, and a single woman fresh
out of prison shouldn't be experiencing scorching ménages with her
three sexy-as-sin cowboys. But JJ's love for her men continues to grow
as she gives into the fevered heat and scorching passions she feels for
each of them.
Life is perfect.

Until her new life is tested when mysterious happenings occur on the ranch and then one of her cowboys is viciously attacked and injured.

Will JJ's newfound freedom and happiness be ripped away?

Rafe, Brady and Dan never expected to find an attractive and very appealing female to help them out at their secluded ranch. But in the wilds of Northern Ontario, female companionship is rare. It's a good thing the three men like to share...

Brady, Dan and Rafe have never been happier. Their cattle ranch is flourishing and their continued desire to share the sexy woman who cares for them makes their life complete. Until danger threatens to rip everything apart...

Loving Her Cowboys

COWBOYS ONLINE 3 ~ Moose Ranch

Jan Springer

After spending ten years in a maximum-security prison Jennifer Jane (JJ) Watson got early parole and a job on a remote Canadian cattle ranch playing housekeeper to three of the sexiest cowboys she's ever met...

Her love for her cowboys continues to grow as she gives into fevered heat. But JJ's simmering restlessness explodes and she's seriously making up for lost time by pursuing her dreams. There's only one little problem. She hasn't revealed to her bosses what she's been up to while they're away tending to the cattle. She knows when they discover her secret, there will be hell to pay.

Ranchers Rafe, Dan and Brady have found the woman who completes them. She makes their secluded ranch a home-sweet-home. She's vulnerable, sweet and willing to share her bed with all three of them. But when JJ's secret is unwittingly revealed, they're stunned and angry. They figure it's time to dole out some fiery punishment in some mighty naughty ways...

Cowboys In Her Heart
Cowboys Online 4 ~ Moose Ranch
Jan Springer

*After spending ten years in a maximum-security prison, JJ gets
unexpected parole and a job on a Canadian ranch serving up scrumptious
dinners and lots of hot love to three of the sexiest cowboys she's ever met.
Jennifer Jane "JJ" Watson has never been happier. She's going to have a
baby!*

Thankfully their wilderness ranch is a nice distraction for her three sexy cowboys while she's away flying her plane. But when she's home, her dominant hunks are tending to her naughty pregnant cravings and that includes plenty of sizzling ménages.

Rafe, Brady and Dan don't much like the idea of their woman flying the Canadian skies and being at the mercy of the unpredictable Northern Ontario weather. They would prefer having her warming their beds twenty-four seven. But she has a way of getting what she wants and right now she needs her new-found freedom.

Worst fears are realized when JJ, her friend and JJ's plane suddenly go missing and she doesn't come back home to them.

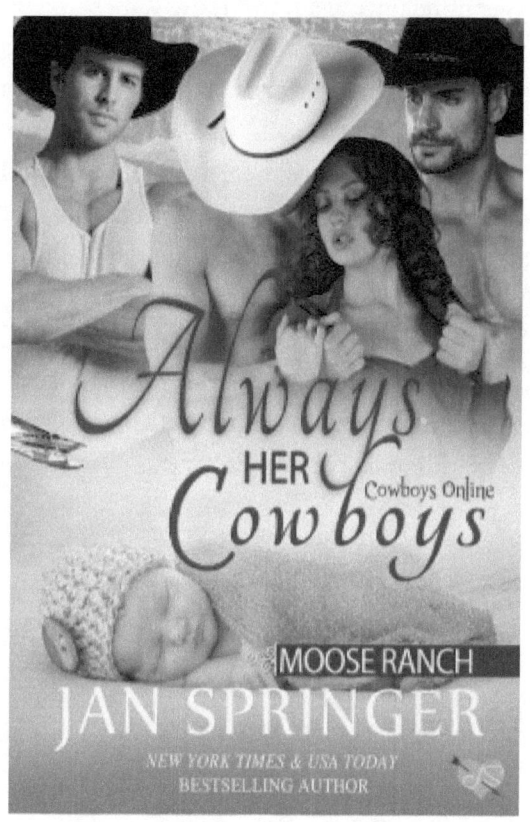

Always Her Cowboys
Cowboys Online 5 ~ Moose Ranch
Jan Springer

Jennifer Jane (JJ) Watson has spent ten Christmases in a maximum-security prison. The last thing she expects is to get early parole, along with a job on a remote Canadian cattle ranch serving Christmas holiday dinners to three of the sexiest cowboys she's ever met!

Rafe, Brady and Dan thought they were getting male ex-cons to help out around their secluded ranch, but instead they get an attractive and very appealing female. In the snowbound wilds of Northern Ontario, female companionship is rare. It's a good thing the three men like to share...

Christmas is coming once again to Moose Ranch and with the due date of JJ's baby approaching fast, JJ is distracting herself from anxiety attacks by keeping herself ultra-busy preparing for the arrival of her baby and planning Moose Ranch's first annual Christmas party!
In having a wee baby on the way, there's a lot of stress for Brady, Rafe and Dan. Especially due to JJ's decision on having a wilderness mid-wife deliver the baby at the ranch house - *with* all *of them present for the birth*! But their concerns don't stop the men from showing JJ how much they love her...out of bed and in!
With wicked snowstorms, a grounded bush plane, a cheerful holiday party and a sweet little baby, the owners of Moose Ranch know this will be one sparkling Christmas season they won't soon forget...

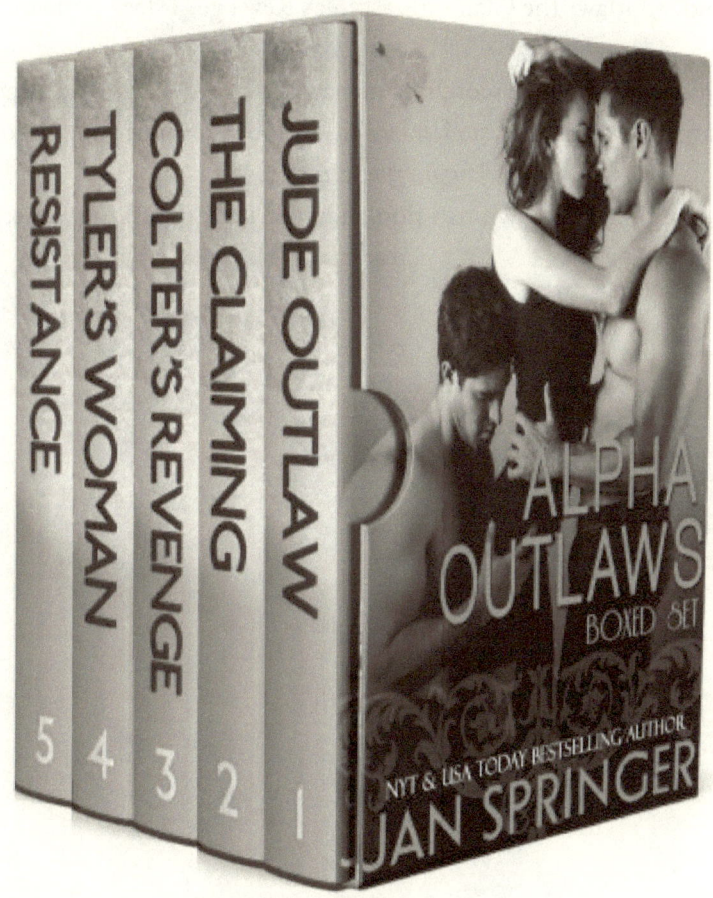

Alpha Outlaws Boxed Set
The Outlaw Lovers (Books 1 - 5)
A fast-acting virus has killed a majority of the world's female population.
With so few women on Earth, a new law is created. The Claiming Law
allow groups of men to stake a claim on a female—as their sensual
property.
The Outlaw brothers have full intentions of declaring ownership of the
women they love...and they'll do it any way they can.
This boxed set contains the first FIVE books in The Outlaw Lovers
series.

Jude Outlaw, The Claiming, Colter's Revenge, Tyler's Woman,
Resistance,
Some scenes include scorching ménages, romances, light bondage,
bdsm, m/f/m/m, m/f, m/f/m, m/m, anal, oral, double penetration,
figging, and more...
Please note: Tyler's Woman Book 4 in this series is not for sensitive
readers.

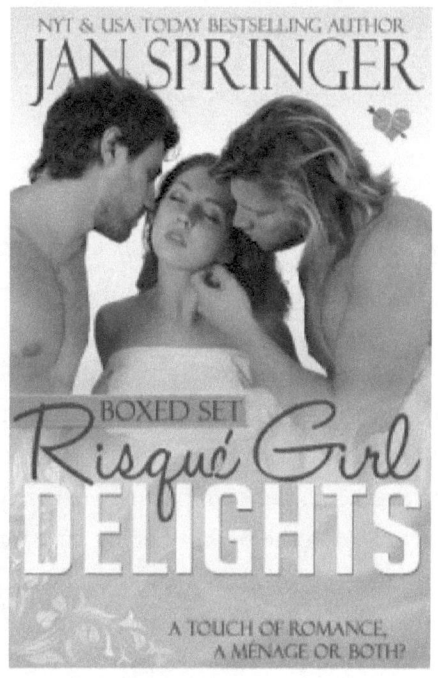

Risqué Girl Delights Box Set
A sizzling set of 4 contemporary erotic romances...Four women dare
to step out of the norm in the Risqué Girl Delights Boxed Set.
Includes sexy romances, naughty ménages, toys and hot alpha males.
Books: Edible Delights, Toygasm, Shy Girl, plus Roman & Julietta.

Edible Delights
Years ago Allie Masters lost herself in the scorching passion of a
ménage a trois relationship with her two bosses. In order to regain her
independence, she walked away.
Max and Nick were very fulfilled with their gorgeous assistant. The
lovemaking was breathtaking and both men willingly shared the
woman they wanted to spend the rest of their lives with. Then she left.

Now Max and Nick have decided it's time to seduce Allie back into their lives.

Toygasm

It's a case of mistaken identity when the two owners of Sexy Toys, show up for an erotic several day photo shoot of their toys with famous nude model Cammie Creek.

Cammie believes the two hunks are the male models she's supposed to work with. Usually she doesn't mix business with pleasure, but when they're seducing her right there in front of the camera, she can't resist turning them into her own personal naughty toys.

Josh and Jode are enjoying the perks of being male models; hot lust, sizzling toys and the best pleasure they've ever had. But how will Cammie react when she discovers they're actually her bosses and not just male models?

Shy Girl

Finally free of an abusive relationship, "Shy Girl" Emma McCall sheds her inhibitions and explores her sensual side at Club Rendezvous, a club specializing in the Alternate Lifestyle.

At the club she's surprised to find Logan Masters, a sexy hunk she's secretly fantasized about since college. With Logan's help, Emma will experience her ultimate fantasy - a scorching ménage a trois.

Roman and Julietta
Her perfect lover...

Modern day pirate Julietta Black's life has always been immersed in the violent and traditional ways of piracy. When her family's arch enemy puts a hit out on her family, Julietta knows there's only one way to lift the hit; she must kidnap the enemy's sexy grandson and force a union between the two warring families. Night after night, wrapped in Roman's strong arms, she can't deny the searing attraction blazing between them. Nor can she deny he now holds her heart as well as her life in his hands.

His dream angel...

When Roman Prince's mysterious captor offers him a luscious woman to bed, fierce desire ignites, melting his usually tight self-control. Lust quickly turns to love as he enjoys their naughty trysts more than he should. How will he react when he discovers he's been kidnapped, not for a ransom, but captured for his sperm?

Naughty Girl Desires Boxed Set:
Romance, Contemporary Romance, Romance Suspense, Box Set
(m/f only)

What You'll Find Inside Naughty Girl Desires
Jade's Fantasy
Kidnap Fantasies 1
Jan Springer
*In the land of the rich and famous, Kidnap Fantasies is the answer to
discreet naughty downtime.*
When ex-downhill skier Jade Hart's two sisters give her a Kidnap
Fantasies questionnaire, Jade is aroused at the prospect of having
no-strings fun in the sun with a stranger whose only job would be to

fulfill her every intimate fantasy. Although she knows she's too shy to send it in, she secretly pours her deepest wishes into the questionnaire. Soon the questionnaire mysteriously vanishes and Jade's fantasy man appears on her luxury yacht in the form of a sexy handy man who gives her an intimate toy-filled Christmas holiday she'll never forget.

Wrapped in red-hot lust for revenge, Avery plots to murder the man responsible for the death of her son.

Her plans are dashed when her ex-husband crashes her wedding and whisks her away on his motorcycle to the rustic Canadian wilderness cabin they'd once honeymooned.

Police detective, Mason is fighting for Avery's love with everything he has.

Armed with whipped cream, handcuffs and his undying devotion, Mason vows he will make Avery love again.

But it's only a matter of time before the man she'd planned to kill hunts them down...

The Biker and The Bride
Jan Springer

Wrapped in red-hot lust for revenge, Avery plots to murder the man responsible for the death of her son.

Her plans are dashed when her ex-husband crashes her wedding and whisks her away on his motorcycle to the rustic Canadian wilderness cabin they'd once honeymooned.

Police detective, Mason is fighting for Avery's love with everything he has.

Armed with whipped cream, handcuffs and his undying devotion, Mason vows he will make Avery love again.

But it's only a matter of time before the man she'd planned to kill hunts them down...

Sinderella Sexy
Jan Springer
By day, she's a dedicated gynecologist.
By night, Dr. Ella Cinder, escapes reality by secretly performing in her
own erotic, adult version of Cinderella, aptly re-titled Sinderella.
When sexy colleague Dr. Roarke Stephenson shows up in the
Sinderella audience on the same night her Prince Charming stands her
up, Ella seizes the opportunity to make Roarke into her Prince
Charming for one carnal night of extremely naughty fun in front of an
audience.
But at the strike of midnight, Ella knows she must face the harsh
reality that Roarke must never learn her secret life and they can never
be together again. Until then, she'll make sure he'll never forget their
night of sensual play.
Dr. Roarke Stephenson is immediately captured by the lusciously
curvy actress who hides behind a mask and is known only as
Sinderella. For some insane reason she reminds him of his klutzy
co-worker, Ella. But that's not possible. Ella would never have the
nerve to do the wickedly delicious things Sinderella does to him, or
would she?

Nice Girl Naughty
Jan Springer
Blind since nineteen, Summer has blossomed into a famous wood
carver. When she's almost killed by a serial killer, she's whisked away to
a secluded wilderness cabin by the man she once secretly loved.

Summer can't get enough of touching professional bodyguard Nick Cassidy's thick, powerful muscles and all those other hard, yummy male body parts that she has always longed to explore.

For years Nick has stayed away from his best friend's kid sister, nice girl Summer. Now he's back, and sweeping his gorgeous redhead into the naughty cravings he's always had for her. With passion blinding him, Nick doesn't realize their hideout isn't safe—until it's too late.

Please note: The titles in Naughty Girl Desires have been previously published.

Pleasure Bound Box Set
The Complete Series
Books 1 - 6

A Futuristic Adult Romance
Books 1-6
This Pleasure Bound Boxed Set is an erotic romance and includes the
first six books in the Pleasure Bound series.
TOP-SECRET MISSION: Explore a recently discovered planet in
outer space.
DISCOVERY: A sizzling trip into the realms of bondage, bdsm,
pleasure-pain, betrayal and...love.
Inside this Boxed Set:
During a top-secret mission to a newly discovered planet, the six Hero
siblings are thrust into a sensual world of erotic violence,
unconventional romance and sizzling sex.
A HERO'S WELCOME

Pleasure Bound Book One
Jan Springer
Being shot and held captive isn't what astronaut Joe Hero had in mind when he agreed to a top-secret mission to explore a newly discovered planet for NASA.
But a man would have to be dead not to fall for the sensual female doctor in charge of his care.
One night of scorching passion in the arms of the stranger from another planet is enough to convince Dr. Annie there's more to males than she's been taught by the Educators.
Who is this sexy hunk and why does she welcome him into her bed and her heart *every* chance she gets?
A HERO ESCAPES
Pleasure Bound Book Two
Jan Springer
Queen Jacey has always fantasized about bedding a male.
But taking one for her enjoyment is strictly forbidden. That is, until an attractive well-hung stranger from another planet forces her to overcome her training and her beliefs.
Being held captive and forced to mate with a gorgeous Queen isn't exactly what astronaut Ben Hero expected when he agreed to explore a newly discovered planet for NASA.
Escaping *should* be his top priority but making sizzling love to Jacey *is* all he can think about.
When he discovers she's also being held captive, Ben's protective instincts kick in big time.
Suddenly they're on the run, irresistibly aroused, and wrapped in each other's arms every chance they get!
A HERO BETRAYED
Pleasure Bound Book Three
Jan Springer

Astronaut Buck Hero didn't count on being held captive or becoming infected with passion poison when he agreed to explore a newly discovered planet for NASA.

If he doesn't get the cure soon he's going to be one *very* dead man. Fugitive on-the-run Virgin has just rescued an infected male and needs to administer the cure - a twenty-four-hour sex marathon. Then she'll turn him over to his enemies in order to gain her freedom.

But her well-laid plans go into orbit when she discovers she's fallen in love with the stranger from another world.

A HERO'S KISS
Pleasure Bound Book Four
Jan Springer

During a secret NASA mission to locate their brothers on the faraway planet of Paradise, the Hero sisters become separated after they crash land...and find unexpected romance with the tormented male warriors of the species.

Jarod and Piper

Being injured and infected by sensuous swamp water isn't what Piper Hero signed up for when she agreed to search for her three missing brothers. But when she's rescued by a dangerously sexy man who makes her so hot that she can't even think straight, Piper is glad that she came.

Jarod Ellis has sworn off women. But he's captivated by Piper Hero, a woman who claims to be related to the Earthmen he has vowed to protect with his life. Although he mistrusts her, she sets free a carnal inferno of needs he's never experienced during his previous life as a pleasure slave.

Despite her intimate fantasies coming true, Piper knows she needs to continue her mission of reuniting her siblings and she'll do it-with or without the help of her well-hung stud...

A HERO WANTED
Pleasure Bound Book Five
(Loosely connected with this series)
Jan Springer

Old-fashioned gal needs a man who loves to walk in the rain. Must be well-hung. A homebody, white picket fence-type of guy. Sexual requirements-gentle yet untamed lover. He must be sexually adventurous who will train me to be same. Must be romantic, enjoy toys, interested in mutual light bondage, ménages are welcome.

That's what full-figured, antiques shop owner Jenna MacLean wants when she and her best friend outline a want ad just for fun on their weekly girls' night out.

After years of being away from his pretty-plus sized ex-girlfriend, Sully's back in town. When he finds the want ad, he knows he's the only man who can make all of Jenna's sizzling-hot fantasies come true. She's never left his heart and he needs her back in his bed-but he's not going the traditional romantic route. This time, he'll prove he loves her with help from the notorious Ménage Club, a relationship club designed specifically to get estranged couples back together with the help of a third and sometimes a fourth in the bedroom.

CAPTIVE HEROES
Pleasure Bound Book Six
Jan Springer

During a secret NASA mission to locate their brothers on the faraway planet of Paradise, the Hero sisters become separated after they crash land...and find unexpected romance with the tormented alien male warriors of the species in this ultra-long scifi book.

Taylor and Kayla

While searching for her brothers, Kayla Hero is bound and imprisoned by the Breeders— along with a male captive whose tantalizing scars pique her interest. Forced to escape with him, she's irresistibly aroused when she suddenly becomes *his* captive.

Wild lust flares in Kayla's eyes— a sensual side effect of the Fever Swamp water she's accidentally ingested. Taylor knows he will enjoy administering the cure — lots of sizzling hot lovemaking!

Blackie and Kinley

Injured and lost in a dense jungle, Kinley Hero is intimidated by the scarred man who hunts her, especially due to the power of erotic submission he holds over her.

Capturing his beautiful female prey, Blackie can't wait to train her as a pleasure slave for the Death Valley Boys. When her captor slips a collar around her neck, Kinley must struggle with lust as a natural submissive.

Shades of Ménage Boxed Set: Four Book Romance Ménage
Collection
A fast-acting virus has killed a majority of the world's female
population. Women's rights are stripped away and The Claiming Law
is created, allowing groups of men to stake a claim on a female—as
their sensual property.
After five years of fighting in the Terrorist Wars, the Outlaw brothers
are coming home to declare ownership on the women they love...and
they'll do it any way they can in Jude Outlaw and The Claiming.
PLUS
In the future...for population control, each human is embedded with a
microchip that supresses the urge to mate.
Centuries later...A rebel group of young doctors are secretly tampering
with their microchips and experimenting with intimacy. Now they
search for allies who can help them with their cause – to eventually

free humanity in the Dystopian Romance Ménage stories "Perfect" & "Imperfect".

Spunky Girl Publishing Erotica
~Jasmine Black~

A BDSM Medical Fetish Erotica Quickie MFM
Waitress Jean Spelling, visits her controversial doctor once a month
for some much-needed...stress relief. She looks forward to putting her
feet up in the stirrups and enjoys Dr. Ball's naughty unconventional
treatments. This time when she arrives, she's surprised to discover that
she'll be physically examined by two doctors and they'll prescribe her
some much-needed release right there on the examination table!

Other Jasmine Black eBooks
Taken by Two Firefighters
Taken by Two Bikers
Taken by Two Billionaires
Taken by Two Bosses

Taken by Two Cowboys
Taken by Two Personal Trainers
Taken by Two Carpenters
Taken by Three Bikers
Taken by Three Billionaires

Jasmine Black Website ~ http://www.jasmine-black.com
Twitter ~ @blackerotica1

For more Jan Springer stories, please visit http://www.janspringer.com

Jan's Newsletter

Hi! If you would like to get an email when my books are released, you can sign up here:

Newsletter: http://ymlp.com/xguembmugmgb

Your emails will never be shared and you can unsubscribe whenever you like.

About the Author

Jan Springer writes full-time at her home nestled in cottage country, Ontario, Canada. She enjoys hiking, kayaking, gardening, reading and writing. She is a member of the Writers Union of Canada, Romance Writers of America. She loves hearing from her readers.

A Word From The Author

Hi! Thank you for purchasing this book. Word of mouth is important for any author to succeed. If you enjoyed this story feel free to leave a short review at the place where you bought it. I would really appreciate it. I look forward to bringing you more stories in the near future. Thanks!

Here are other ways we can connect:
Jan Springer Website at http://www.janspringer.com
Instagram – http://www.instagram.com/janspringerauthor
Facebook - https://www.facebook.com/janspringereroticromance
Twitter - https://twitter.com/janspringer @janspringer
Pinterest - http://www.pinterest.com/janspringer1/
Jan's Blog - http://janspringerauthor.wordpress.com/blog-2/
LinkedIn - http://ca.linkedin.com/in/janspringerauthor/
Google Plus - https://plus.google.com/u/0/
101527334949931513035/posts
Jan's Newsletter - http://ymlp.com/xguembmugmgb
Goodreads - https://www.goodreads.com/author/show/
260628.Jan_Springer
Happy Reading,
jan springer

Don't miss out!

Visit the website below and you can sign up to receive emails whenever Jan Springer publishes a new book. There's no charge and no obligation.

https://books2read.com/r/B-A-WGQ-JAMK

BOOKS 2 READ

Connecting independent readers to independent writers.